By Popular Demand

The most anticipated love story at *St Piran's Hospital*!

ST PIRAN'S: THE WEDDING! by Alison Roberts

Devilishly handsome Dr Josh O'Hara and beautiful, fragile
Megan Phillips have a secret that once ripped them apart.
But now, under the warmth of the Cornish sun, the most
unlikely of happy endings finally has its chance…

And if you've missed any of the stories
in our fabulous *St Piran's Hospital* series,
why not go back to where it all began…?

**These books are available in eBook format
from www.millsandboon.co.uk**

Dear Reader

Two years ago I had the pleasure of being part of the *St Piran's Hospital* series.

I loved my story about Luke and Anna, and adding to the conflict of the characters Josh and Megan, whose tense relationship ran throughout each of the stories in the *St Piran's* series.

When the series finished, it certainly looked as if these two star-crossed lovers could never get a happy ending of their own. Not only was there a wife still in the picture but, shockingly, she was now pregnant! I was honoured to be asked to revisit St Piran's and find a happy ending for Josh and Megan, but I also thought: Hmm…this will be quite a challenge. Challenge is a good thing, I reminded myself. It takes us out of our comfort zone and makes us stretch our wings and achieve more than we might have thought we could. And isn't it true that the more you put into something, the more you get out of it?

I really hope you love this story as much as I did in the end.

Happy reading!

With love

Alison

ST PIRAN'S: THE WEDDING!

BY
ALISON ROBERTS

MILLS
BOON

First published in Great Britain 2013
by Mills & Boon, an imprint of Harlequin (UK) Limited.
Large Print edition 2013
Harlequin (UK) Limited, Eton House,
18-24 Paradise Road, Richmond, Surrey TW9 1SR

© Harlequin Books S.A. 2013

Special thanks and acknowledgement are given
to Alison Roberts for her contribution to the
St Piran's Hospital series

ISBN: 978 0 263 23129 8

Alison Roberts lives in Christchurch, New Zealand, and has written over 60 Mills & Boon® Medical Romances™. As a qualified paramedic, she has personal experience of the drama and emotion to be found in the world of medical professionals, and loves to weave stories with this rich background—especially when they can have a happy ending. When Alison is not writing, you'll find her indulging her passion for dancing or spending time with her friends (including Molly the dog) and her daughter Becky, who has grown up to become a brilliant artist. She also loves to travel, hates housework, and considers it a triumph when the flowers outnumber the weeds in her garden.

Recent titles by Alison Roberts:

MAYBE THIS CHRISTMAS...?
THE LEGENDARY PLAYBOY SURGEON**
FALLING FOR HER IMPOSSIBLE BOSS**
SYDNEY HARBOUR HOSPITAL:
  ZOE'S BABY*
ST PIRAN'S:
  THE BROODING HEART SURGEON†

*Sydney Harbour Hospital
†St Piran's Hospital
**Heartbreakers of St Patrick's Hospital

These books are also available in eBook format from www.millsandboon.co.uk

PROLOGUE

'CODE ONE, DR Phillips.' The registrar slammed down the phone as he swung his head. 'Theatre Three.'

Megan's pager began sounding at precisely the same moment, with the particular sound reserved for an absolute emergency.

The surge of adrenaline made everything else irrelevant. Even signing her resignation. Her ticket to finally escape.

She dropped her pen on top of the paperwork and leapt to her feet.

'Let's go.'

A code one was a life-threatening emergency. A life was at stake. More than one life, potentially, if Megan was being summoned. For a paediatrician to be called in with the same paging system used for something like a cardiac arrest meant that a newborn baby could be in need of specialist resuscitation. For it to be happening in Theatre meant the baby was arriving by emergency Caesarean. There were no scheduled Caesareans for the St Piran's maternity department today so this one must have come in via the emergency department.

The registrar, Matt, was keeping pace with Megan as she ran for the elevator.

'Suspected uterine rupture,' he said.

Megan nodded, holding her finger on the button as if that would speed up the arrival of the lift. Then she turned away.

'Stairs,' she snapped. 'It'll be quicker.'

'She'll be bleeding out, won't she?' Matt was right behind her. 'The baby won't stand much of a chance.'

'Depends.' Megan was taking the stairs two at a time. 'Internal blood loss can sometimes slow down or even stop simply because it's filled the available space and that puts pressure on ruptured vessels. The real danger comes when you open that space and release the pressure.' She blew out a hard breath as she pushed open the fire stop door on the theatre suite level. 'But you're right. It's critical for both of them.'

The main corridor in St Piran's theatre suite

was deceptively quiet. The flashing orange light above the door of Theatre Three was a beacon. But so was something else that Megan hadn't expected to see.

A lone figure, at the end of the corridor, in front of the tall windows. A figure that stopped pacing and was now poised, reminding her of a wild animal sensing danger.

There was no mistaking the intensity of the stare Megan knew was directed at her.

'Get some scrubs on,' she ordered Matt as they reached the door to the change rooms. 'Then go in and make sure we've got everything we might need on the resus trolley. Check the incubator. I'll be right there.'

The figure was moving towards her. It might only be a silhouette because of the background light of the fading day beyond the windows but Megan knew exactly who it was.

Josh O'Hara.

Oh…*God*…

Why now? When she'd successfully avoided being alone with him for months.

Ever since that final, devastating kiss.

She could have avoided it now, too. Why

hadn't she gone straight into Theatre with her registrar?

Because there was only one reason why Josh would be pacing the corridor like this. Why he wouldn't be in the Theatre with a case that would have been in his emergency department only minutes ago.

Megan was holding her breath. She'd never seen Josh look this tense. Distraught, even. Not even when he'd come to tell her that he loved her but they had no future.

Or…maybe she had. Once. So long ago now that the memory of his face was only a faint chord in the symphony that nightmare had been.

They'd had more than one turning point in their star-crossed history, she and Josh.

Clearly, this was another one. The third.

Bad things came in threes, didn't they?

That meant that this had to be the last. Of course it was, because escape was only days away for Megan now. She'd be on the other side of the world very soon. Just not quite soon enough.

Megan sucked in enough air to be able to speak. 'It's Rebecca, isn't it?'

His wife. They might not be living together as man and wife at the moment but they were still married.

A single nod from Josh. God, he looked terrible. He always looked like he could use a shave but right now his face was so pale it looked like he hadn't been near a razor for a week. And he must have been virtually scrubbing at his hair with his fingers for it to look so dishevelled. The expression in his eyes was worst of all, however. Blue fire that was born of desperation. Guilt. Despair.

And shame, perhaps, for what he had to beg for?

'The babies…' The words came out strangled. 'Please, Megan. Do your best for them. They… they won't let me in.'

Of course they wouldn't. He was far too emotionally involved. This was his family in Theatre Three. The whole family. As if it hadn't been hard enough for Megan that Rebecca was going to give him a child, she had to go one step further and present him with a complete family. Two babies.

And it might be up to her to save the lives of Josh's children.

The irony would be unbearable if she gave herself even a moment to think of it. Fortunately, she didn't have a moment to spare. As if any reminder of the urgency was needed, her registrar burst out of the changing room and went into the theatre.

Even then, something made Megan hesitate for just a heartbeat and, without any conscious thought, she reached out to touch Josh's arm in a gesture of reassurance. Not that she needed to touch him to ramp up the tension. Megan opened her mouth to say something but there were no words available.

With a curt nod, she turned away and went to throw on some scrubs.

Of course she would do everything she could to save his family. She would do it for any of her patients but if heroics were called for in this case, she wouldn't hesitate.

After all, it was Josh who had saved *her* life all those years ago.

* * *

That touch on his arm was almost enough to utterly unravel Josh.

His breathing ragged, tiny sounds escaping that could have been the precursors of gut-wrenching sobs if he couldn't pull himself together, Josh went back to his pacing.

Back to the window end of the corridor where he was far enough away to keep his agony private but close enough to see who came and went from Theatre Three.

He got his breathing back under control and silent again but guilt was still threatening to crush him.

This was his fault. If Rebecca died, he would know where the blame could be laid. Why had he allowed himself to be pushed so far away? In recent weeks she had refused to see him. Or talk to him even. The only information he had been given had been that Rebecca was 'fine'. That her GP was looking after her, with the implication that he was doing a better job than Josh ever had.

God…if it hadn't been so hard, he would have been able to ask the questions that might have told him something wasn't right. He might have given in to the urge to turn up on her doorstep and make sure she was 'fine' for himself.

As recently as this morning, he'd thought of doing exactly that on his way to work but it had been all too easy to talk himself out of it. He hadn't really wanted to start his day by stopping by his old house, had he? If he was really honest, he wanted to avoid laying hands on the woman he'd once loved but should never have married.

But the way he felt about Megan had been the reason he'd married Rebecca at all, wasn't it?

Oh…*God*…the threads of his life were so tangled. So confused… The pain of his childhood, knowing how much his mother had loved his father and seeing how she'd been destroyed bit by bit as she had been cheated on time and again. The conviction that, if this was what love was all about, he wanted nothing to do with it.

Knowing that he was falling deeper in love with Megan with every passing minute of that night they'd spent together.

Turning his back on her and everything that that kind of love could lead to.

Marrying Rebecca because he had been lonely.

And because it had been safe. He had liked her. Respected her. Loved her the way you could love a good friend. A *safe* kind of love.

Had he allowed himself to be pushed so far out of Rebecca's life because it had been so hard to face the irrefutable evidence that he'd cheated on Megan by having sex with Rebecca that one, last time? When he'd known the marriage was over and it was only a matter of time before he and Megan could finally be together.

But Megan believed he had cheated on his wife when he'd gone to *her* bed.

He couldn't blame her for hating him for it.

At least he'd had the chance to save Megan's life that time, ironically in not dissimilar circumstances, but right now he'd been rendered useless. He couldn't even try to save Rebecca.

Did people think he wouldn't *want* to?

She was the mother of his children, for God's sake. Still his wife, even if it was in name only.

He had loved her once.

Just…not the way he'd loved Megan.

A part of him, so ruthlessly and successfully squashed months ago, was still capable of reminding him that he still loved Megan in that way. And always would. Not that Josh was going to acknowledge the whisper from his soul. It was a love he had chosen to forsake.

For his career and his sanity, that first time.

The second time it had been for his unborn children.

What would he have left if things weren't going well in Theatre Three?

He'd lose his wife.

His children.

And he knew what that pain was like. It was years ago now but the memory of holding that tiny scrap of humanity in his hands would never leave him. He'd known, on some level, that it had been his own son that Megan had lost that day. That he had been holding. It was too neat a fit, not only with the dates but with the power of that night. The connection that had felt like it would last for ever. The kind of connection that made it feel right to create a baby. Make a family.

He'd lose Megan again, too, if things weren't going well in Theatre Three.

No. A fresh wave of pain ramped up the confused agony Josh was grappling with.

He'd already lost Megan. Months ago.

* * *

Something made him stop the caged-in prowl back and forth across the corridor end. Made him freeze and whip his head sideways.

Of course it was Megan. In green theatre scrubs now, with her hair covered by a cap. Moving decisively from the door of the changing room to the one beneath the flashing orange light. She didn't look in his direction.

Despite, or perhaps because of, the overwhelming emotions he was having to deal with, Josh allowed himself to be distracted from the agonising, lonely wait for just a heartbeat.

Baggy, shapeless clothes like theatre scrubs did nothing to stop Megan being the most beautiful woman Josh had ever known. It didn't matter what she wore. Scrubs. Tattered old jeans. The gorgeous gown she had worn as a bridesmaid in a royal wedding party.

Oh…no…Tasha. Josh reached for the mobile phone clipped to his belt. He needed to let his sister know what was happening. She could be the one to break the news to their mother.

What time would it be in San Saverre?

As if it mattered. Tasha would want to know

the trouble that both her brother and her best friend were in right now.

Her loyalty would be tested. She knew the empty space he was in now, having sacrificed a relationship with the woman he truly loved for the sake of his children. To keep a marriage, even in name only, so that he wouldn't repeat history by being the kind of man their father had been. She would know how devastating it would be, being faced with the prospect of losing those children.

But she would also know how hard this had to be for Megan. To be expected to save his babies that were being carried by another woman. The babies she could never have given him because losing *their* son, all those years ago, meant she could never have another child.

Josh had to stifle an audible groan.

He was a reasonably intelligent man. He was damned good at the job he did, running the emergency department of St Piran's.

How was it that he always messed things up so badly when it came to his relationships with women?

He could save lives.

But he was just as good at breaking hearts.

It was his fault Rebecca hadn't had medical help in time to prevent this catastrophe.

His fault that Megan had become pregnant with his first child.

His fault that she'd lost the baby. That she'd never have another.

No wonder Megan had blanked him at Tasha's wedding. He'd done it to her, hadn't he?

Twice.

Every time he'd come to a point in his life where he was losing control…faced with the absolute vulnerability of loving someone—*Megan*—enough to give them the power to make or break him…he had frozen. Backed away and stayed with what he knew. What seemed to work.

He was an emotional coward.

Or a control freak?

As a modus operandi it was fine as far as his career went. Kept him on top. Moving forward. He could deal with a thousand people professionally and win acclaim. But he didn't seem to be able to deal with even one person on an intimate level and not cause serious harm.

What made anybody think he would be a good father?

Maybe he'd end up just like his own father had been. Worse than useless.

Maybe he would fail *all* his children before they even had a chance of life.

No.

The word was wrenched from deep inside Josh.

These babies couldn't die.

Megan wouldn't let them.

The baby looked dead.

Delivered to Megan's area of the theatre seemingly within seconds of the emergency surgery starting, the nurse laid her limp burden down under the lights, gave the paediatric team a grim glance and moved swiftly back towards the main table. Another baby would be delivered almost as quickly.

The resuscitation protocol was automatic for Megan. Airway, breathing, circulation, drugs.

She couldn't allow the fact that this was Josh's baby anywhere near the conscious part of her brain. Even a hint of distraction, let alone panic, could be disastrous.

'Suction,' she ordered.

Making sure the newborn's head was at the correct angle to keep the airway open and holding the end of the soft tubing at a length that couldn't go too far and trigger a laryngeal spasm, Megan cleared away any possible obstruction. Against the soft chugging of the suction machine, Matt was gently stimulating the baby's body by rubbing the skin with a warmed towel.

To one side of them, the tension was escalating.

'Pressure's dropping again.' The anaesthetist's tone was a sharp warning. 'Ectopic activity increasing.'

'We've got to get this second baby out. Where the hell's the suction? I can't see a damned thing...'

On Megan's side of the theatre the baby was showing no signs of starting to breathe.

'Bag mask.' Megan's order was clipped.

With the tiny mask covering both the mouth and nose of the infant, she gently depressed the soft bag to deliver the tiny amount of air needed to inflate the lungs. Again. And again.

'Not pinking up,' Matt noted.

'He's in shock.' Megan signalled for a technician to take over the bag mask. 'Start chest compressions, Matt.'

'You going to intubate?' Matt was already slipping his hands around the tiny chest, keeping his thumbs in front ready to start compressions.

'In a minute.' Megan could see over her registrar's shoulder. The second baby was lying on a towel a nurse was holding flat on both hands as the cord was cut. She was close enough to be able to see if there were any signs of life.

There weren't.

They needed a second paediatric team in here but there hadn't been one available. It was up to Megan and Matt here. At least they had a second resuscitation trolley set up.

'Keep up the CPR,' she instructed Matt. 'One hundred and twenty beats per minute. He may need some adrenaline. We'll need to cannulate the umbilical vein as well as soon as we can. Let's see where we are with baby two.'

Baby two was a girl. Just as flat as her brother was.

Or maybe she wasn't. After the first puff or

two of air from the bag mask, the tiny girl gave a gasp and began trying to breathe on her own. It wasn't enough, though. The heart rate was still falling.

At ten minutes the Apgar score for both babies was still unacceptably low. They needed intubation, stabilisation and transfer to PICU—the neonatal intensive care unit.

They were both alive, however, and Megan was fighting to keep them that way.

The battle on the other side of Theatre Three was not going so well.

Part of Megan's brain was registering the increasing tension as she slid a small tube down the first baby's airway to secure ventilation. The obstetric surgeon had found the torn abdominal artery but too much blood had been lost. The fluid replacement and the drugs being used were not enough. Rebecca's heart had stopped.

CPR continued on the mother as Megan checked the settings on both incubators and watched the recordings being taken on both babies reach a level that meant it was safe to transfer them to PICU.

As the second incubator was wheeled from the

theatre, she heard the defeated note in the surgeon's voice.

'Time of death…sixteen forty-three.'

November in Cornwall could provide a bone-chillingly grey day with an ominous cloud cover that threatened a torrential downpour at any moment.

The rain held off for the duration of Rebecca O'Hara's funeral but the background was suitably grim for the final farewell of a young mother who had never had the chance to see her babies.

'I hope nobody gets too sick today,' somebody muttered as the congregation filed into the chapel. 'Looks like practically the entire staff of St Piran's is here.'

There were whispered conversations in every pew.

'Who's that sitting beside Josh?'

'Tasha. His sister. The one that married the prince. I didn't know she was pregnant.'

'No. On the other side. The older woman. Is that his mother?'

'Yes. Her name's Claire. I heard that she's

planning to move to Penhally to help him look after the babies.'

Further up the aisle, St Piran's CEO, Albert White, was sitting with a member of the board of directors, Luke Davenport.

'Thank goodness the babies are doing so well,' he muttered. 'Josh looks wrecked enough as it is.'

'It's all so sad.' Luke's wife, Anna, tightened her grip on her husband's hand. 'All of it. Rebecca was so unhappy for so long. I think she really believed that the babies would make everything all right.'

She exchanged a glance with her husband. One that suggested that—given enough time—maybe things would be all right eventually.

For Josh, anyway.

At the very back of the church, a woman noted for her tendency to gossip wasn't about to rely on meaningful glances.

'You'll see,' she muttered to the colleague sitting beside her. 'Now that the wife's out of the way, he'll be married to his fancy piece in no time flat. You just wait and see.'

'Shut up, Rita,' her companion hissed.

For once, Rita did shut up. She spent the next few minutes watching as the final people squeezed in to take up the last of the standing room at the back of the church. She'd been watching the congregation ever since she'd arrived. Early.

'Where *is* Megan?' Rita finally had to ask. The organ music was fading and the funeral director was taking his place to start the service.

'Haven't you heard?' The person on the other side seemed amused that Rita was out of the grapevine loop for once. 'She left St Piran's yesterday.'

'Where's she gone?'

'Africa.'

'She's coming back, though…isn't she?'

'Doubt it. Her resignation was permanent. She's joined *Medécins San Frontières*.'

'But—'

'*Shhh.* Leave it, Rita. It's over.'

CHAPTER ONE

Almost two years later

WHY ON EARTH had she come back here?

Penhally, Cornwall, on this November day seemed grim. Grey and bleak.

And so *cold*. Megan was quite sure the temperature was a single digit and having come from an African summer where a cool day could still be thirty degrees Centigrade, this was like being inside a fridge.

It didn't help that she'd lost so much weight in recent weeks, of course. Dengue fever took a huge toll, especially the second time around. Her old coat hung so loosely on her that Megan could wrap it around her body like a blanket. Which was exactly what she did as she stood there, shivering, a suitcase by her feet, looking out over Penhally Bay as the taxi disappeared down the hill.

The sky was a deep, ominous grey and looked ready to unleash a torrent of rain at any minute. The sea looked equally menacing with whitecaps on the steel-grey water, moored yachts rocking on the swells and huge breakers crashing onto dark, wet sand. Seagulls circled overhead and the sharp, plaintiff notes of their cries echoed perfectly how Megan was feeling.

It was too cold to stand here in the street, that was for sure, but the view as she turned towards the cottage was just as dispiriting. The gate was barely visible in the wild growth of what had been a neatly trimmed hedge. The small garden was a wilderness but not high enough to disguise the coils of long-dead plants in the hanging baskets on either side of the front door or the broken panes in the lattice windows, some of which had curled pieces of cardboard trying to fill the small squares.

How long had it been since the last tenants had gone? Since she'd fired the rental agency who had failed to fix the issues like the broken pipes that had driven the tenants away? At least six months, but Megan had been too far away and too busy to cope with the hassle of putting new arrangements in place. Angered too by the flood of queries coming in from developers who were always waiting in the wings like vultures to get their hands on such a desirable piece of real estate.

And then she'd been too sick.

It was a ridiculously hard effort to push the gate open and drag her suitcase along the flagged path now choked with weeds and the branches of perennials like lavender that looked like they hadn't been cut back since she'd left two years ago. Megan felt the prickle of tears at the back of her eyes. This had all been so pretty once. Not that she'd ever managed to keep it as picture-perfect as her grandmother had but she'd tried her best to keep it the same.

To preserve the memories of how it had been in her childhood, when this cottage and her beloved gran had been the most precious things in her life.

And that, of course, was what had brought her back now.

This was where her roots were.

Not that she'd actually been brought up here. No... After her parents were tragically killed in a car accident, Megan had gone to live with her grandmother in London. But Gran had been brought up in Penhally and that was where she'd taken Megan for a seaside holiday, every summer. They'd rented this very cottage, year after year, and the memories of those weeks had always been tinged with the rosy perfection of being the best time in the best place in the world. The cottage had been the home of her heart for as long as she could remember.

When she'd been so dreadfully ill, nearly losing her life after losing the baby, Megan had been forced to finally tell her grandmother the truth. Despite being already frail, Gran had gathered up all her strength, wrapped it all with the unconditional love she had for her granddaughter and declared that they needed a new beginning, starting with a seaside holiday. When she'd found that their beloved rental cottage was on the market, Gran had simply moved their lives back to her home town and, by doing so, had allowed Megan to put the pieces of her shattered life back together.

So this cottage and its memories, the sea and the village all added up to *home*. And home was the place that drew you back when you needed comfort. A safe place to recover and reassess your life.

Besides, the cottage badly needed sorting out. It would have been unforgiveable to let it crumble into some sort of ruin. Megan could hear the kind of 'tsking' sound her grandmother would have been making as she pushed open a front door stiff with disuse and stepped into a space that felt just as cold as it was outside. A space that reeked of damp and mould and mice.

Oh...*hell*...

This was far worse than she'd expected.

It wasn't just the evidence of appalling neglect. The horrible smell of the rubbish left by the tenants littering the hallway or the ominous sound of trickling water coming from the kitchen. Or was it the bathroom upstairs? Probably both.

It wasn't the knowledge that there would be no electricity on yet and it mightn't even be safe to have it turned back on until she found someone to check the wiring. It wasn't even the wave of incredible weariness as Megan contemplated the energy it would take to sort any of this out.

No. It was the feeling of being so alone.

The result of the emotional punch of the memories of *not* being alone in this house.

Not that Josh had ever stayed here. But this was where it had ended, wasn't it? Her feet seemed to be literally treading memory lane. Taking her down the hallway and into her kitchen while her head and her heart conjured up the figure of Josh following her.

Her feet crunched through pieces of broken glass on the kitchen floor.

Her heart had been broken long ago. How on earth could it still hurt this much?

Because it was here that Josh had prised that jug of water out of her hands? Just before he'd kissed her as if it was the end of the world and she was the only thing that mattered to him.

Here that Josh had told her how much he loved her?

When he'd told her that he couldn't be in love with her any more because his *wife* was pregnant.

She could actually hear echoes of his voice.

I love you so much, which is why this is the hardest thing I've ever had to do...

It was just one night, weeks before you and I...

I love you, Megan...but no child of mine will grow up as I did, without a father. I won't do that. I have to make this work...

Yes. That had been when her heart had really broken. With the realisation that Josh had been lying to her when he'd told her the marriage was over. When she realised he'd still been sleeping with his wife at the time as he'd shared *her* bed.

That was when she'd known that it was truly all over. When any hope had died. She had known that, despite the love they had for each other, they could never, ever be together. Nothing could change that. If Rebecca's death hadn't even made a dent, then being back in Penhally certainly wasn't going to. That sense of betrayal was clearly still there. She'd thought she'd got over it all but the pain she was feeling right now was proof that she'd only managed to hide from it.

The chirrup of her mobile phone announced a text message. It was from Tasha—the only friend she'd really kept in touch with over the last couple of years. Maybe because Tash had also left Penhally. Or because she'd understood. How ironic was it that Tasha was Josh's sister?

U there yet? The message read. *How's it going?*

Megan's breath came out in a snort of wry amusement as she pulled off a woolly glove and tapped a response.

Just got here. Bit messy.

Would Tasha wonder what she was referring to? The house? Her emotional state? Her life?

Maybe she knew. *Hugs,* came back. *U OK?*

I will be. Thnx. Call u soon.

Tasha would be worried about her. Her friend had been dubious about the return. Why not come somewhere sunny to recuperate? she'd suggested. Like San Savarre? Or London, which would be close enough to make sorting things out a little easier and she wouldn't be so alone because Charles would be there, wouldn't he? Being with such a good friend who knew the whole story would be the best protection from being vulnerable to ghosts from the past.

She could cope, Megan had assured Tasha. It wouldn't be for long. Yes, she knew that Josh had moved from the smart St Piran town house he'd shared with Rebecca and was living closer to Penhally now. Of course he had moved. He'd needed a bigger house and a garden for the children and for his mother, who'd gone to live with them. By tacit agreement, she and Tash rarely talked about her brother but in those early days Megan had needed to know that the babies had survived their dramatic entrance to the world and had gone on to thrive. She hadn't really needed the later snippets that had told her Josh was a perfect father to little Max and Brenna. Or that his emergency department at St Piran's hospital was considered to be the best in the county.

Or that there were no women of any significance in his life. That he'd taken some sort of vow not to mess up anybody else's life.

His children and his career were all that mattered to Josh now. He probably wouldn't even be interested that she was visiting the area. There was no reason for their paths to cross other than the fact that this was a small village.

Megan closed her eyes to the view of Penhally Bay she still had in front of her through the kitchen window.

Maybe it was time to really let go of the past. *All* of it.

Sell her grandmother's cottage and move on for ever.

If the memories were this hard to handle, how on earth did she think she would cope if she actually met Josh again?

The sooner she got out of here the better.

Maybe she didn't even need to think about fixing up the cottage. It wasn't as if it would make much difference to the kind of money a developer would be happy to offer.

She did need to find a place to stay for the night, however, and she really didn't want to contact any old friends from St Piran's even though she knew they would be happy to help.

The information centre in the village should be able to direct her to somewhere that would have a room available. Too weary in both body and spirit to face carrying her suitcase, Megan locked it into the cottage, taking only her shoulder bag as she set off to walk down the hill.

When she went back through the gate, however, the small path down to the beach caught her eye.

Just a look, she told herself. A glimpse into part of her past that wasn't associated with Josh. If she could feel the sand beneath her feet and close her eyes and breathe in the salty air, maybe she could remember something happier.

A summer's day, even. Building sandcastles and collecting shells and pieces of seaweed. Sitting on the damp sand with her bare legs stretched out in front of her, waiting for the thrill of the last wash of a wave to foam around her. Running back to the cottage to show Gran her new treasures.

Maybe it should have been running into Josh unexpectedly that she should have prepared herself for.

The dog on the beach was large enough to be quite frightening as he came loping towards Megan with a piece of driftwood clamped between his jaws. In the periphery of her vision, however, Megan could see a woman and children who had to be the dog's family because the beach was otherwise deserted. Nobody with children would have a vicious dog, would they? Besides, his teeth were occupied with the large piece of driftwood. And his tail was wagging in a very friendly manner.

'Crash!' The woman called firmly. 'Come back here.'

Crash? The name was unusual enough to ring a bell. He'd only been a gangly, half-grown puppy then, of course, but Megan could remember him wearing a big, white ribbon around his neck at a summer beach wedding. Luke and Anna Davenport's wedding.

It wasn't Anna coming towards her now, though.

'I'm so sorry.' The woman, bundled up warmly in a coat, hat and huge scarf, was very apologetic. 'He's a bit too friendly, so he is. But he wouldn't hurt a fly.'

She had a strong Irish accent and the lilt took Megan immediately into a space she really didn't want to be. Was everything and everybody here going to make her think instantly of Josh? She took a deep breath and focused on the dog.

'It's fine,' Megan said. 'I don't mind.' To prove it, she scratched the dog behind one of his ears, which was easy to do because Crash was leaning on her leg. 'Isn't this the Davenports' dog?'

'Indeed it is. We mind him during the day

when they're both working. The children love him to bits, so they do.'

The children were half hidden behind folds of the woman's coat as she held their mittened hands. Megan could see cute hats with ears on them and bright plastic boots. A pink pair with red flowers and a green pair with eyes that made them look like frogs. The owner of the frog boots peered out from the folds of coat.

'Cash naughty,' a small voice pronounced.

Crash wagged his tail harder.

The woman looked down to smile at her charges. 'Say hello, children.'

But the children said nothing. Neither did Megan. Her gaze had also dropped and she could see that the children were no bigger than toddlers. That they seemed to be close enough the same size as each other to be twins.

And…oh, God…the cheeky smile on the little boy's face had a charm out of all proportion to his age. His eyes were too dark to determine their colour but they were so…alive. His face danced with mischief and Megan could feel the pull of a personality that went past being cute or attractive.

It was the kind of pull that made it impossible not to get sucked in.

To fall in love.

The kind of connection that could be overwhelming. That had the capability of derailing, if not destroying, a life.

Megan sucked in a deep breath. How ridiculous to be…what, *afraid* of a child?

But it was more than that, wasn't it? Much, much more.

Her gaze jerked up again and now she could see past the folds of the scarf and a woollen hat pulled low over her forehead. She could see a woman who looked to be well into her sixties but could be younger because those lines suggested a life that had not been easy. Behind the spectacles she wore, Megan could now see the colour of her eyes and her heart skipped a beat. She knew who had inherited that shade of indigo blue.

'Oh, my goodness. You're Josh's mother… Claire O'Hara?'

'Indeed I am.' Claire blinked in surprise. 'Have we met?'

'Just once. At the hospital. When the twins

were still in the intensive care unit. The day before…'

The gaze Claire O'Hara directed at Megan was intense. And then it turned distinctly wary. 'Oh…You're Megan Phillips. The doctor. I'm so sorry. I didn't recognise you. It was such a terrible time…the day before poor Rebecca's funeral and…'

'There's no need to apologise.' Megan was still caught by the undertone she couldn't fail to have missed in the older woman's gaze. Recognition of more than her identity.

Had Josh filled her in on his star-crossed lover history?

Unlikely. But this was a small village and St Piran's hospital grapevine was robust thanks to people who loved to gossip, like that dreadful woman—the ward clerk in the NICU…what was her name? Ruth? No…Rita.

Oh…Lord. Had Josh's mother heard about the way they'd met, way back when Megan had been a final-year medical student? That she'd become pregnant after a one-night stand with Josh, who hadn't been remotely interested in seeing her again? That he'd saved her life but that their son had been too premature to survive?

That baby—Stephen—had been Claire's grandson.

Even if she hadn't caught up on ancient history, she couldn't have missed the scandal of the way she and Josh had been drawn back to each other when he'd moved to St Piran's.

"Poor Rebecca", she'd said. Because her daughter-in-law had been badly treated by her husband, who had given up on their marriage and had been more interested in another woman? That Megan was the "other woman"? And that, in the end, they hadn't been able to keep their hands off each other?

Or maybe she felt sorry for Rebecca because she'd died knowing that Josh was only staying in the marriage for the sake of the children.

Megan was acutely embarrassed. Ashamed, even. The way she might have felt if Claire was her own grandmother and she'd disappointed her beyond measure. It had been a mistake to come back here. A dreadful mistake.

Except that Claire wasn't eyeing her as if she was the cause of all her son's troubles. 'And you look…different,' she continued. That wary expression had completely gone now. Claire's face actually creased with a kindly concern. 'You're so pale, dear. Are you all right?'

'I'm…um…fine.' Megan nodded for emphasis and then tried to cover her embarrassment at the undeserved sympathy by looking down and smiling at the children. They stared back, wide-eyed and still shy.

'This is Max.' Claire smiled. She turned her head. 'And this is Brenna.'

They were so impossibly *cute*. Small faces with perfect features and she could see now that their eyes were as blue as their grandmother's and their father's. She wondered if the hair beneath the animal hats would be glossy and black and so soft to run your fingers through it, just like Josh's. Or had they inherited their mother's blondeness?

Josh's children. Josh and Rebecca's children. Living proof that he'd gone back to his wife's bed after his marriage was supposedly over, leaving him morally available to Megan.

Maybe something of how hard this was showed in her face.

'Up,' Brenna demanded, dropping her grand-mother's hand to hold both arms in the air. 'Up, Nan. Pick me *up*.'

Claire had to let go of Max's hand to pick Brenna up. Max immediately toddled off, at some speed, towards the waves. Crash loped after him.

'*Max*. Come back. We have to go home now. It's starting to rain.'

It *was* starting to rain. Big, fat, icy drops of water began pelting the small group on the beach.

Claire tried to put Brenna down to run after Max but the little girl shrieked a protest. Crash had dropped his lump of wood and was circling Max, who looked determined to get closer to the wild surf.

'I'll get him.' Megan dropped her shoulder bag and took off.

It took only seconds to reach the toddler but the burst of energy it took was enough to make Megan feel faint. She really wasn't fine at all, was she?

It was just as well that Max's little legs had

also exhausted their energy reserves. He grinned at Megan. 'Puddle?' he asked hopefully.

Oh, help…he was totally irresistible with that crooked little smile and the hopeful expression on his face.

'Not today, sweetheart.' She scooped up the toddler and held him in her arms. 'It's not sunny enough, is it?'

Her steps almost faltered as she carried the child back to Claire. She was holding Josh's son. The closest she had ever come to holding the child she could have had herself. The shape of the soft little body cuddling into her was delicious. When Max wrapped his arms around her neck to hang on tighter, Megan felt a flash of pain in her chest, as if her heart was cracking. An old scar, perhaps, being torn open?

Thank goodness it was raining. If any tears escaped, at least nobody would know except her. All she wanted was to grab her bag and escape the moment she got back to Claire, but how could she leave her now? The rain was coming down harder and she had to get two small children and a very large dog off the beach and—

presumably—into a car. Or was Josh now living this close to Penhally beach? To her cottage?

'The car's not far,' Claire said. 'Just down the road a bit.' She put Brenna down and took a leash from her coat pocket, which she clipped to Crash's collar. Holding the lead with one hand, she held out her other hand to Brenna. 'Can you walk now, pet?'

'No-o-o. Up.'

Relief that Josh wasn't going to turn out to be a close neighbour made Megan take a deep breath.

'Let me help,' she said. 'You're getting wet and you've got a bit of a handful here.'

'Don't I know it?' Claire picked Brenna up, managing to keep hold of the leash. 'And there I was thinking that it would make my day easy if I gave them all a quick run on the beach before we did our messages in the village. I don't know where these tots get their energy from.'

Megan had to hide a smile as she found herself struggling to keep up with Claire on the way back to the car. Limitless energy was clearly an O'Hara trait.

Not that she could leave Josh's mother to cope alone once they reached the car either. The wind had picked up and was threatening to blow the heavy doors closed and it was a mission to strap two wriggling toddlers into their car seats and then shove a folder double stroller out of the way to make room for a big dog to jump into the back hatch of the station wagon.

Finally, everything seemed to be sorted but as Claire reached up to pull the hatch down, she suddenly stopped. She closed her eyes and bent her head, her breath escaping in almost a groan.

'Are you all right?'

'Oh, I'm fine, I am. Just need to catch my wind.'

But Megan could feel a prickle of awareness. One that she'd learned never to ignore.

'Sit down for a minute,' she said. 'Here...' She pushed the stroller further back and guided Claire to sit on the edge of the car floor. Crash shuffled sideways to make room. The car was pointed into the wind and with the hatch cover still up they were fairly well protected from the weather. 'You are a bit short of puff, aren't you?'

'It's the cold, that's all.'

But Claire was virtually gasping for air. She started loosening the woollen scarf around her neck but abandoned the action to start rubbing the top of her left arm through her coat sleeve.

'Have you got any pain in your chest?' Megan asked.

Claire shook her head. 'It just gets…tight… that's all. In the cold…and…if I hurry.'

'But your arm hurts?'

'Only an ache… It's nothing… Goes away…'

Except it didn't seem to be going away this time. And Claire's face looked grey. Even as Megan watched with mounting alarm, beads of perspiration appeared beneath the edge of the woollen hat.

'Go.' A small voice came over the top of the back seat. 'Go, Nan. Go-o-o…' The plea trailed to a miserable sound. Beside Max, Brenna began to cry.

Claire tried to stand up but had barely begun moving before she collapsed backwards.

'I don't…I don't feel very well…' She tugged harder at her scarf and it came away and rippled to the ground.

'Do you have any history of heart problems?' Megan asked. 'Do you carry spray for angina or anything?'

'No…I'm fine…' Claire's face was crumpling. She looked terribly afraid. 'I *have* to be,' she whispered.

Megan had stripped off her gloves and was feeling for Claire's pulse. The rapid, uneven beat made it very clear what had to be done. She reached for her shoulder bag to find her mobile phone.

'I'm calling an ambulance,' she told Claire calmly. 'You need medical attention.'

'No…I'll be fine… Just give me…a minute…'

But the emergency services had answered Megan's call with commendable swiftness and she was already describing their location.

'Cardiac chest pain,' she told the dispatcher. 'Radiating to the left arm. Arrhythmia.'

'You're a doctor?' the dispatcher queried.

'Yes.'

'An ambulance is on its way. Are you able to stay with the patient?'

In case of a cardiac arrest?

'Of course.'

Megan made Claire as comfortable as she could while they waited for the ambulance. She took off her own coat to provide the older woman with some extra warmth. Picking up the scarf, she saw why it had been difficult for Clair to loosen. It had become caught on a necklace chain, which had broken.

Not that she pointed that out to Claire but, to prevent a possible treasure being lost, she put the chain into her own coat pocket, leaving the scarf in the back of the car. Her actions were brisk and organised but automatic because she was busy providing as much reassurance as she could, knowing that any stress could make this much worse. If Claire was, as she suspected, having a heart attack, then anxiety could tip the balance and stop her heart completely.

Would she have the strength herself to keep up CPR until an ambulance arrived?

Thank goodness she didn't need to find out. The ambulance arrived only minutes later and the crew had Claire on a stretcher and attached to a monitor within a very short time. She had an oxygen mask on by the time the rhythm settled on the screen of the life pack and a paramedic was preparing to insert an IV line.

'Marked ST elevation,' her crew partner noted. 'Looks like an infarct all right.'

'Are you on any medication?' the paramedic asked Claire. 'Are you allergic to anything that you know of? Have you had any aspirin today?'

Claire was shaking her head in response to all the questions. Things were happening too fast for her to find any words. The children in the car were both crying loudly now but Megan was still holding Claire's hand.

'It's going to be fine,' she reassured Claire yet again. 'These people are going to look after you and make sure you get checked out properly at hospital.' She turned to one of the crew members. 'Claire's son is Josh O'Hara at St Piran's. He may well be on duty at the moment so you might like to let him know in advance who you're bringing in.'

'Will do.'

Megan tried to let go of Claire's hand but the grip tightened. She leaned closer to hear the words that were being muffled by the oxygen mask.

'But who's going to…look after the children?'

Megan felt a cold chill run down her spine. No. She couldn't offer to do that. It would be too hard. The scars were still too fresh. Best not to go near anything that might pick at them. Her life was taking a new direction now. Having it derailed would be a disaster.

The paramedic was busy with her other hand. 'Sharp scratch coming, Mrs O'Hara.' She slid a cannula into a vein. 'There. All done.'

Claire lifted the hand that Megan was still holding, trying to pull the oxygen mask away from her face. 'I can't do this…the children…'

Her partner was leaning over Megan. 'Chew up this aspirin for me,' he instructed Claire. 'I'll give you a sip of water to wash it down.'

Megan was in the way. She tried to pull her hand free but Claire's grip tightened.

'Please…' Claire's face looked alarmingly grey. Getting stressed was making her condition rapidly worse. 'Can't you help?'

'Yeah…' The paramedic gave Claire a very direct glance. 'Can you drive?'

'Yes, but—'

'You could follow behind the ambulance, then. I'm sure there'd be someone else to look after Doc O'Hara's kids once you got there.'

Claire was nodding. 'Please, Megan…'

'Otherwise we'll have to bring them in the

ambulance. Or wait for back-up.' The paramedic was sounding impatient now. 'And we really need to get going.' The look he gave Megan was a direct warning. Hold this process up any further and if anything goes wrong between here and the emergency department of St Piran's, she would have contributed.

Megan was caught. She couldn't walk away. There were two crew members in the ambulance and one of them had to drive. If the other had to care for two toddlers, there would be nobody left to care for Claire. And she could get worse. Go into a cardiac arrest, even.

Her nod was jerky. 'I'll do it,' she said tightly. 'Are the keys in the car?'

'Yes…oh…*thank* you, lovie.' Claire finally let go of her hand but her eyes filled and tears rolled down her cheeks.

Megan closed her eyes for a heartbeat. There was no help for this, so all she could was do her best to cope with it. At least she had a kind of advantage here. She knew there was a high likelihood that she would have to see Josh and she would have a few minutes to at least try and prepare herself emotionally for that.

No doubt Josh would prefer to avoid this encounter as much as she would. And he probably wouldn't have the luxury of any warning.

Megan opened her eyes and smiled at Claire. 'Try not to worry,' she told her. 'I'll be right behind the ambulance. I won't let anything happen to the children. You'll see them again very soon, I promise.'

The back door of the ambulance slammed behind her after Megan had climbed out.

The vehicle was pulling out onto the road as Megan checked the fastenings on the car seats, fastened her own safety belt and started the car, surprised to see how shaky her hands were.

The beacons on the ambulance were flashing and the siren began to wail as the vehicle picked up speed. Megan wasn't going to try and keep up with it. Not on a wet road when she was feeling shaky. Certainly not with two precious children in the car.

She didn't need to follow that closely anyway.

The route to St Piran's was written on her heart, like everything else about this place.

CHAPTER TWO

'INCOMING, DR O'HARA.' The nurse's voice came from just behind Josh's shoulder as he scrolled through the images on the computer screen.

He grunted an acknowledgement, still focused on the screen. Surely something had shown up on the MRI of his earlier patient to explain her acute neurological symptoms?

'Status two.' The nurse sounded oddly nervous but, then, she was new and had only just learned that flirting with him was likely to earn disfavour. 'Sixty-year-old woman who looks like she's having an infarct.'

'Put her straight into Resus, then. Is Ben around?'

'Yes…but…'

The back of Josh's neck prickled as he turned his head. 'But what?'

'The patient is your mother, Dr O'Hara.'

The prickle ran down the entire length of his

spine now, turning icy cold. Josh was on his feet and moving before he gave the action any conscious thought.

'How far away?'

'ETA five minutes. They're coming from Penhally.'

They? Were the children in the ambulance as well? This couldn't be happening. Not now, when his life was exactly the way it was supposed to be. The children, the house, his job—none of it would have been possible without his mother's help.

An infarct? Claire O'Hara had never had a day's illness in her life. She'd never smoked. She was as slim now as she'd been in her twenties. Her blood pressure was fine. She had energy to burn.

Or did she? Had she been pushed too far by him taking up the amazing offer of her helping him to raise the twins?

If this was yet another disaster in his life, could the blame be laid, yet again, at *his* feet?

Ben Carter, another emergency medicine consultant at St Piran's, was already in the resuscitation area. The defibrillator was being tested.

A twelve-lead ECG machine was standing by. He glanced up and saw Josh.

'Don't panic,' he said quietly. 'We don't know exactly what we're dealing with yet.'

'Status two infarct,' Josh snapped. 'Unstable. What the hell happened? Have you had any details? Where was she? Did she...*arrest* somewhere?'

'No. That much I do know. She's status two because she's throwing off a few ectopics. She's on oxygen and she's had aspirin, GTN and morphine. Her breathing's improving.'

'Improving? My God, how bad *was* it?'

'Josh...' Ben stepped closer to put a hand on his colleague's arm. 'I've got this, OK? It'll be good for Claire if you're here but you need to stay calm.'

'What about the children? Were they with her?'

'I don't know.' Ben was looking past Josh now. Towards the double doors sliding open to admit a stretcher and ambulance crew. A nurse was pointing them towards the resus room. He turned to a nurse. 'Has the cardiology registrar been paged?'

'Forget the registrar,' Josh said. 'Get Anna Davenport down here. This is my *mother*, for God's sake.'

Claire looked terrified as she was wheeled into the resus room.

'Josh...' she gasped, reaching out a hand. 'Thank heavens you're here.'

'Of course I'm here.' Josh took hold of the hand. He knew he was getting in the way as the ambulance crew transferred Claire to the bed and gave Ben a handover but, for the first time in years, his mother needed *him* instead of the other way round. He kept his eyes on her face as the staff stripped away the clothing from her upper body and started adding extra dots so they could take a more comprehensive recording of the electrical activity in her heart. Ben was drawing off bloods for urgent analysis.

'Let's sit you up a little bit, Mrs O'Hara,' a nurse said, slipping another pillow behind Claire. 'And I'm just switching the oxygen over to this plug on the ceiling so we can get rid of the portable tank. No, don't take your mask off.'

Claire ignored the nurse, pushing the mask clear of her mouth. 'The twins, Josh...they're...'

'Please keep your mask on.' The nurse gently moved Claire's hand. 'It's important that you get some oxygen at the moment.'

'I can hear you.' Josh leaned closer. 'What about the twins?'

'They're fine.' The paramedic was loading the portable oxygen cylinder back onto the stretcher. 'The doctor who called the ambulance for Mrs O'Hara said she'd be bringing them straight here. She can't be far behind us.'

'A doctor?' Josh was confused. 'Was she at the medical centre?' Getting treatment, even, for some condition she'd never let him know she had?

'No. She was at the beach. With the children and a big dog.'

'Crash. Oh, no...' The woman coming swiftly into the resus room sounded as though she was starting a conversation with an old friend. 'What's he been up to now, Claire?' She was smiling down at her patient. 'More importantly, what on earth have you been up to?'

The smile was reassuring but Josh could see the concern in the face of the head of the cardiology department. Concern that increased as a technician handed her the sheet of paper from the twelve-lead ECG machine. Ben was also reading the ECG over her shoulder.

'What is it?' Josh forgot his confusion about a doctor being on scene when Claire had become ill. He hadn't missed the significant glance passing between Anna and Ben.

'Left anterior,' Anna said calmly. 'ST elevation of up to three millimetres. Have we got anything back on the bloods yet? Cardiac enzymes? TNT?'

Josh had to take a deep breath as he heard Ben relay the earliest results. He didn't want to let Claire know how serious this could be. An infarct that knocked out part of the left ventricle was more likely to have serious consequences. Every minute counted now so that they could save as much cardiac function as possible.

Anna had turned to Claire. 'You're having a heart attack, Claire,' she said gently. 'But there are things we can do to minimise the damage it might be doing to your heart. I'm going to take you up to the catheter laboratory and we can see exactly where the blockage is in your coronary arteries. We'll clear it if we can and might put something called a stent in to keep the artery open.'

'You're going to…operate on me?' Claire's face was as white as the pillow behind her.

'Not exactly. You'll be awake. We put a tiny tube inside an artery and that goes into your heart. It's very clever.'

'And Anna's very good at it,' Ben put in. 'You'll be in the best hands, Claire.'

'We'll give you a sedative,' Anna added. 'You'll be awake but it won't hurt and we won't let you get too anxious.'

'No.' Claire shook her head. She tried to peer past the medical team crowded around her bed. 'I can't go. Not yet. She said I'd see the children again. Very soon.'

'*Who* said?' Josh could feel the tension of this whole situation spiralling upwards. They couldn't let Claire get any more upset because there was still a definite risk of her rhythm degenerating into a fatal arrhythmia. Who had his children? Where were they?

'She does.' Claire's lips were trembling. 'The doctor.'

'*What* doctor?'

'The one who…looked after them…when they were born.'

'Megan Phillips? But that's impossible. She's in Africa.'

'Not any more.'

Josh froze as he heard the voice coming from behind Ben and Anna on the other side of the bed. Everybody turned to see who was at the entrance to the room. Holding the handles of the double stroller that contained the twins.

'*Daddy.*' Both Max and Brenna's faces lit up with smiles as they spotted their father. They held up four little arms.

But Josh didn't even see the plea. His gaze was locked on the woman behind the stroller.

Oh, my God…

Megan.

For just a heartbeat, the world stood absolutely still.

Nothing else mattered.

That his mother was dangerously unwell. That he had two tiny, defenceless children calling for him. That he was the head of a department of St Piran's Hospital that was gaining widespread recognition as a centre of excellence in emergency medicine.

None of those things could even exist in the space Josh was sucked into for just a second.

A space of such intensity, it pulled the oxygen from the air around him and made it feel impossible for him to breathe.

The space he'd been in on that New Year's Eve party when he'd met Megan properly for the first time. When he'd sensed the power of truly falling in love. The power that had held his mother captive and broken her life.

He'd been there again in the trauma of that emergency when it had looked as though Megan might die. When he'd sensed the power of what a parent's love for a child could be as well, and had vowed never to let that power control him either.

During the course of that one, incredible night when he'd shared her bed for only the second time—just before he'd found out he was going to become a father.

On the day he'd had to do the hardest thing in his life, and tell her it was all over.

In that moment when he'd had to beg her to

do her best to save the lives of Rebecca's and his children.

Daddy.

The echo of the word penetrated the space. Grounded Josh instantly. He was where he needed to be. Living his life the way it had to be lived.

The way he *wanted* to live it.

Nothing could be allowed to change that. Somehow, he had to resist the incredible pull that that space could exert. It felt like his life was depending on it. It was almost ironic to have his mother in the same room. The example he'd grown up with of the damage that that kind of love could inflict.

Stepping towards the newcomers, Josh was aware of the tension around him. The kind that came from a collective holding of breath, waiting to see what was going to happen.

Their story was hardly a secret, was it? Not that Anna or Ben knew that he'd slept with Megan while he'd still been married. While his wife had been in the early stages of pregnancy with the twins. But everybody knew their early history by now. And if anybody had missed the way they'd been drawn back to each other when he'd first come to St Piran's, the hospital grapevine would have filled them in. Maybe everybody *did* know about that night in the on-call room.

Oh…Lord…Tash knew everything. How much did his mother know?

Josh pulled the barriers of his professional image around him like a force field.

'Megan… What a stroke of luck you were there for my mother when she got sick. And thank you so much for taking care of my children.'

He stooped to release the safety straps around the twins. Not that he squatted down fast enough to miss the change of expression on Megan's face. Had she been holding her breath like everyone else in here? Hurt by his deliberate focus on his own family? Himself?

He hadn't even asked her how she was despite some alarm bell ringing faintly in the back of his head. As he stood up, with a twin under each arm, he couldn't help taking another look at her. That warning bell hadn't been a false alarm. She looked…terrible.

So thin. So pale. Something was wrong. Her

emerald-green eyes looked dull enough to be frightening.

Except that Josh had no right to have an emotional stake in Megan's wellbeing any more.

And even if he did, this wasn't the time. Or place.

He held her gaze for the briefest moment, however. He couldn't help it. He knew his concern would be transparent but that didn't matter either. He tried to send a silent message.

We'll talk. Soon.

'The babies…' Claire's voice wobbled. 'Let me give them a kiss before I have to go.'

Megan's heart was hammering in her chest.

How ironic would it be if she provided another cardiac emergency for Josh to deal with?

What had she expected to happen here? A moment of pure fantasy where the existence of anyone else—including his mother and children and colleagues—simply evaporated? And Josh's face changing as though he was witnessing a miracle? That he would come towards her in slow motion and sweep her into his arms? Kiss her again just like he had that last time…?

Maybe some tiny, secret part of her had hoped exactly that.

It didn't mean that she'd wanted it to happen, though. Or that she could have coped with going down that track. It was the last thing she wanted when she'd fought so hard to find her new direction. A completely different track.

Josh had done exactly the right thing. Been professional. Cold, almost. But then, when she'd been trying to process that, feeling dizzy and bewildered, he'd looked at her again. *Really* looked at her. And she'd known that this wasn't it. This moment couldn't count as their first meeting after a long absence.

That had been postponed due to unforeseen circumstances.

Circumstances that were slightly chaotic right now, as staff bustled around, taking care of Claire and preparing to move her to the catheter laboratory even as Josh gave her the chance to kiss and cuddle each of the children. Max grabbed one of the wires attaching an electrode to the cardiac monitor and pulled it free, which set off an alarm. The sound frightened Brenna, who clung to her father and had to be persuaded to give her grandmother a quick kiss.

Meanwhile, Megan simply stood there, clutching the handles of the stroller. She could hardly walk out, could she? Not when these people were old friends. How rude would it seem to Ben and Anna if she just left?

Besides, she felt frozen. Watching Josh. Seeing the easy way he held his small children and talked to them. Knowing that his light tone and smile was an act. That the way those lines had deepened around his eyes advertised how much stress he was under right now.

And…he looked as gorgeous as he ever had. His palpable charm hadn't changed either and it was being directed towards the twins right now and they looked as if they were being won over by that lazy smile as easily as she always had. He must have raked his fingers through his hair a fair few times to get it looking so rumpled, and to her horror Megan could feel the urge to smooth it with her own hands. To push that wayward lock back from his forehead and cup his face with both her hands so that she could really look and discover every tiny change that time had wrought.

She gripped the moulded plastic handles of the stroller more tightly. Forced herself to smile in response to Ben's greeting.

'We'll have to catch up. I'd love to hear about Africa. You here for a while?'

No. She needed to escape as fast as she could.

'I…I'm not sure yet.'

Ben's pager sounded and he excused himself hurriedly. Megan wished she had one clipped to her own belt. A reason to disappear.

But she couldn't leave quite yet. Anna needed to know that her dog was locked in the back of Claire's car out in the car park and the cardiac surgeon had been busy on the phone for the last few minutes, juggling her responsibilities so that she could join the cardiologists and be involved in this emergency angioplasty case.

Anna finished her call and nodded at someone. A loud clicking noise announced that they had disengaged the brake on Claire's bed. It was time to move.

'You coming up with us, Josh?' Anna queried.

'Not that you can stay in the cath lab, of course, but you're welcome to come in while we set up.'

Ben stuck his head back into the room.

'You're covered here, mate. Give me a call later and we'll sort out what happens tomorrow.' He smiled at Claire. 'I'll come up and see you in the ward later. You'll be feeling a lot better by then.'

Josh stood there, holding a twin on each hip.

Megan stood there, holding the handles of the empty stroller.

As Ben vanished, Josh's gaze shifted to settle on Megan.

So did Anna's.

The whole room seemed to pause and the atmosphere was electric. Josh couldn't take the twins with him to go with his mother. Everybody was clearly waiting for her to make an offer to help out.

It was too much to ask. Way too much. Josh had plenty of staff here, didn't he? Any number of nurses who would probably fight for the chance to earn his appreciation by babysitting.

But Josh was looking at her and it was like

that graze of a glance he'd given her when he'd picked the twins up. The one that recognised *her*.

Not as a separate person.

As part of what they had once been. Together.

With a huge effort Megan broke the eye contact as she tried to marshal the wild tumble of thoughts and emotions in her head. She looked at Anna.

'I've got Crash outside in Claire's car,' she said. 'What would you like me to do with him?'

'Oh…help…' Anna caught her bottom lip with her teeth.

'Sorry, love.' The beeping of the monitor recording Claire's heart rate increased its tempo noticeably. 'It's my fault. I took him to the big beach for a run with the twins and—'

'It's OK.' Anna's gaze flicked to the monitor. 'Don't you worry about anything, Claire. I can sort this. Oh, help…if only Luke hadn't left already. I could have called him to take Crash *and* the twins home.'

'Did Luke decide to go, then?'

Josh had moved towards Megan. He put Max down and began fitting Brenna back into the stroller. Max turned around and headed back towards Claire's bed.

'Not so fast, cowboy.' Anna scooped the toddler up and came towards the stroller as well. She was close to Megan again, but her gaze was on Josh. 'Yes,' she told him. 'He'll be halfway to New Zealand by now.'

Megan blinked. New Zealand? This whole situation was starting to feel surreal. Anna noticed her expression.

'Luke's father has had a stroke. It doesn't sound too bad but his mother is freaking out completely. When he checked flights late last night, he found he could get a ticket for a dawn flight leaving Heathrow. He drove to London at one a.m.'

'Of course he wants to support his mother. I'll think of something else.' But the desperate note in Josh's voice was so uncharacteristic it told Megan just how tightly he was hanging on here. Did he feel like his world was collapsing around him?

His mother was seriously ill.

His ex-lover had appeared in his life again.

He had a child-care issue on his hands.

Who could he turn to?

Another silence. Megan couldn't ignore the trouble Josh was in here.

Just because he'd broken her heart…because they could never be together…it didn't mean that she had to stop caring, did it?

Even if it did, it didn't mean that she was capable of stopping.

'I can look after them,' she said quietly. 'All of them.'

Both Josh and Anna's faces lightened instantly.

'I couldn't ask you—'

'Would you really?' Anna spoke over Josh's exclamation.

'I can't take them home, though,' Megan added. 'My cottage is a bit…uninhabitable at the moment.'

'Take them to my place,' Anna suggested. 'The key's just upstairs in my office. You know where our cottage is, don't you?'

'Yes. You had your wedding on the beach just down the hill.'

Josh was shaking his head. 'It would be better

to take the twins home. My keys are right here. And they might be happier if they have their own stuff around.'

Meaning that they might not want to be with her? A complete stranger?

The look Josh gave her was apologetic. As if he was reading her mind.

'I mean, there's all their toys. And the food they like. And their PJs and beds if things don't…'

The unspoken warning that things might not go as well as expected was enough to make them all suddenly anxious to get going.

'Fine.' Megan nodded. 'I'll take them home to your place, Josh. Only…'

He turned his head, already moving to go and find his house keys.

'Only I don't know where you live.'

'Anna can fill you in.' Josh kept going.

Anna smiled. 'That's easy. Josh bought the Gallaghers' farm, next door to my place. On the St Piran side. Crash has a basket on the veranda. He won't wander—it's always been his second home.'

Josh was back, thrusting a set of keys into Megan's hand.

'Thank you *so* much.' Stooping swiftly, he touched the twins' heads. 'Be good for Megan,' he told them. 'I'll be home soon.'

Claire's bed was moving past them now, with most of the staff disappearing as well. Any moment now and Megan would find herself alone with Josh's children and the keys to his house in her hand.

How surreal this all was had just gone off the Richter scale. Was she the only person who found this unbelievably bizarre?

No. Claire was watching Megan as her bed was manoeuvred through the door of the resus room. There was concern in her face. And sympathy? Something else as well.

Maybe a message. One that said: *You can do this. We all know how strong you are.*

It wasn't true. Nobody around here knew how strong she had become over the last two years. Maybe if she'd had that kind of strength way back, none of this would have happened, but at least she had it now.

She *could* do this.

And if she succeeded, it would prove to everyone just how far she had moved on with her life.

She could prove it to Josh.

She could prove it to herself?

CHAPTER THREE

How weird was this?

To be going home to his children, knowing that Megan Phillips was there. Looking after Max and Brenna, like a stand-in mother.

In his house.

Like a stand-in wife?

No.

Josh wasn't going into that space. The idea of he and Megan being together had died a long, long time ago.

The moment he'd told her that Rebecca was pregnant.

Parking his car next to where the family wagon was, Josh walked towards the rambling, old farmhouse that looked out over the ocean. It was far too dark and drizzly to see anything, especially in the welcoming glow of the house lights, but he could hear the sea and the wash of waves was a familiar, comforting pulse of sound.

Crash was on the veranda. Watching. Ready to protect his second home from any intruder. His tail began waving as soon as Josh climbed the steps, however, and a damp nose nudged his hand in welcome.

He let the big dog into the house with him as he entered.

Josh knew he needed some moral support. He just didn't realise how much until he walked inside and could smell hot food and hear the sound of voices and could feel…

Could feel Megan's presence in his house. Even before he entered the big, open-plan living area where the children were snuggled up on the couch on either side of Megan, listening to a story.

Josh had to pause for a moment. To listen to the soft lilt of Megan's voice. To soak in the tilt of her head and the way his children were tucked into the crooks of her arms as if it was the most familiar, and loved, place in the world for them.

Dear Lord…if things had been different…it could have been *their* son listening to Megan reading that story. Getting sleepy and needing to be tucked up in bed. Leaving his parents to have a quiet evening together bathed in that flickering firelight.

That soul-deep yearning had been successfully buried for years now.

But it hadn't gone away, had it?

Perhaps it was fortunate that Crash didn't get stopped in his tracks and mesmerised the way Josh had been. The dog padded far enough into the room to interrupt the story.

'*Cash.*' Max wriggled free of Megan's arm and slid down from the couch, running to throw his arms around the big animal.

'*Daddy.*' Brenna also wriggled free and made straight for Josh, who was glad of the need to move and pick his daughter up. He had to give her a good cuddle and kiss as well and that covered a few more awkward seconds. And when he looked up, Megan's gaze was on Crash.

'Sorry,' she said. 'I didn't realise he was allowed inside. I shouldn't have left him out in the cold like that.'

'That's his spot,' Josh assured her. 'It means Anna can drop him off or collect him without worrying about disturbing us.'

Us.

God…it sounded as if he was including Megan.

'She'll be here to pick him up soon,' he added hurriedly. 'She had a few things to catch up on and wanted to check on Mum again.'

'How is she? Did James get to see her in the end?'

Josh nodded. 'Yes. He agrees that bypass surgery isn't necessary. Anna put in four stents and everything's looking great. The damage should be minimal and Mum will be able to come home in a day or two.'

'That's wonderful.'

'Yes. I'm sorry it all took so long, though.'

'No worries. You said it might.'

He hadn't thought it would take this long, though. That phone call to update Megan on progress and fill her in on what the children might need had been hours ago.

'Thank you so much,' he said now. 'I don't know how we would have managed it you hadn't been there.'

Megan turned her head away. 'I'm sure you would have managed just fine.'

Of course they would have.

Just like Josh had managed when Megan had

finally walked out of his life, physically, months after her emotional departure.

Just when he'd needed her most.

'When did you get back from Africa?'

'Today.' Megan turned back, a wry smile shaping her mouth.

Welcome home.

The words hung there, unspoken.

Josh cleared his throat. 'Max, don't let Crash lick your face, mate. Come on…it's high time you two were in bed.'

Megan closed the story book and put it on the table beside the couch. 'I'll leave you to it.'

Josh had scooped up Max as well. He had to peer over two small heads to catch Megan's gaze.

'Couldn't you stay for a few more minutes…?' He had barely had the chance to thank her properly, let alone talk about anything other than today's drama. He should let her leave but… His mouth seemed to be moving of its own accord. Producing words that weren't getting filtered through any of the usual channels.

'For a coffee or something?' he was saying. 'To… I don't know… I don't feel like we've even said hello yet.'

A long pause this time, during which Megan got slowly to her feet.

Was it his imagination or did she close her eyes and dip her head a fraction, almost as if she was praying for strength?

Whatever it was, it lasted only a heartbeat and then she spoke very quietly.

'I'll put the kettle on, then.'

Megan was sitting at the kitchen table with a half-empty mug by the time Josh returned.

'Sorry. That took a bit longer than usual. I think they're missing their gran.'

Megan smiled. 'I'm sure she's missing them as well. They're…gorgeous kids, Josh.'

'They are, aren't they?' He tried not to sound too full of pride as he went to the mug on the bench beside the kettle.

'I didn't finish making your coffee.' Megan was watching him. 'I didn't know whether you still took it black or…or if you'd started having sugar or something.'

'Same old,' Josh said lightly. 'Some things never change, do they?'

Their eye contact was fleeting but significant.

Things *did* change over time. Little things, like how you had your coffee. Big things, like how you lived your life.

Megan was looking around as if she was trying to find a way of changing the subject.

'This place is wonderful. I'd never have thought of you living on a farm, though.'

Did she think of him, then? Josh found it unexpectedly hard to take his next breath. His chest felt tight with some nameless emotion. Relief? *Hope*? He fought to shake it off.

'It's not a farm any more. Doug Gallagher died suddenly eighteen months ago and June decided to sell up.' He poured boiling water into his mug. 'The neighbours on the other side wanted the land but not the house so she subdivided. We've only got about three acres or so around the house. More like a big garden than a farm.'

'Must be perfect for the kids with all this space and the beach just across the road.'

'Seems to work well.' Josh sat down at the end of the table, at a right angle to Megan.

It felt too close.

It didn't feel close enough.

He had to close his eyes for a moment. To focus and get through the wave of confusion.

'It is perfect,' he heard himself saying aloud. 'I'm lucky enough to have the perfect life.' Who was he trying to convince here? Megan or himself? 'It's a bit further away from work than the apartment,' he added, 'but that was no place to try and raise children.'

'No.' The mention of the St Piran's townhouse he had shared with Rebecca had chilled the atmosphere, and Megan's tone, noticeably. Or had it been his declaration that he had the perfect life? One that didn't contain her? Maybe he'd gone too far in erecting protective boundaries.

'I needed to get away, anyway,' Josh added quietly. 'To make a fresh start.'

Megan seemed to be finding the colour of her remaining coffee fascinating. 'As you do,' she murmured.

The tiny silence couldn't be allowed to continue because anything could have taken root and flourished enough to get spoken aloud. Things like…

I've missed you. So, so much.

It would be much safer to stick to less personal topics but there was something personal that Josh couldn't ignore any longer.

'Are you OK, Megan?' Oh, help…the query sounded far too intimate. Dangerous territory. He had to back off fast. 'Physically, I mean?'

He couldn't read the glance he received in response. Women were so good at that. Making you feel like you couldn't have stuffed your foot any further into your mouth if you'd tried.

'I'm getting over a rather nasty bout of dengue fever. Second one in a six-month period.'

'Sounds horrible.'

'It's certainly not pleasant. I'm having a bit more trouble getting my energy level back this time. And I'm still getting a bit of joint pain.'

Josh didn't like that. It made him feel like he did when one of the twins got sick. Or fell over and skinned a knee. The feeling of needing to make it better.

'Do you need anything? Anti-inflammatories or…multivitamins or something?'

Megan shook her head. 'I'm fine, Josh. I just need a bit of time, that's all.' She glanced up and her face was amused. 'I'm a doctor, remember? I can look after myself.'

The amusement made her face more alive. Brought a hint to her eyes of the kind of sparkle they used to have. Josh wanted to keep it there.

'Doctors make the world's worst patients,' he reminded her with mock severity. 'Sometimes they have to be told exactly what they should be doing.'

To his disappointment, the amusement faded from Megan's eyes and she sighed. 'I *have* been told,' she said sadly. 'That's the only reason I left Africa.'

'The *only* reason?' The question popped out before Josh could stop it and it earned him another one of those inscrutable looks.

'I need to sort my cottage out. It's turned into a bit of a mess.'

How ridiculous was it to feel disappointed? What had he expected? That Megan would say she'd come back because she'd wanted to see *him*? He wouldn't have wanted that, anyway.

Would he?

A wave of something like confusion made Josh's next query tentative. 'Are you planning to live in it again?'

'No.' The head shake was decisive. 'But renting it out hasn't worked out so well. I might have to sell up.'

And then she'd have no ties to Penhally left at all. That was a good thing.

Wasn't it?

'Where will you go?' Josh could feel himself frowning. 'Back to Africa?'

'I can't. Not if I stay with MSF, at least.'

'Why not?'

'I've got immunity to two types of dengue fever now. I'm also female and Caucasian. It puts me in a high-risk bracket to get the haemorrhagic form of dengue and that can be fatal. It's not a risk that MSF is prepared to let their medical staff take.'

Josh felt his gut tighten. 'Surely it's not a risk *you'd* be prepared to take either?'

Megan's silence spoke volumes. She wanted to go back, that much was crystal clear.

Why? What would make anyone want to risk their lives like that? Something was nagging at the back of Josh's mind. A cryptic conversation he'd had with Tash a while back. Not that they ever talked about Megan these days—he'd made sure it had been a no-go subject ever since the wedding—but she'd said something about how happy Megan was finally. And she'd had a smile that suggested…

'Is there someone in Africa?' Josh heard himself ask. 'Someone…special?'

'You could say that.' Megan nodded and she had the same sort of smile on her face he remembered Tash having. A…loving kind of smile.

Josh had to look away. He gulped down a mouthful of coffee and tried to think of something…*anything*…to change the subject.

He didn't want to hear about the new love of Megan's life.

It was good that she was happy.

It wasn't as if either of them would ever consider being together. Not now.

Josh had to regain control of what was happening here. Of his life. He'd almost lost it today, what with his mother's health scare.

With seeing Megan again.

But the shock was wearing off. Those odd frissons of confusion were fading. Knowing that

Megan had moved on to someone else should be all he needed to put things back into perspective.

To help him remember what it had been like two years ago.

There was anger in the mix, deep down, wasn't there? Anger that Megan had not believed him when he'd said that his marriage was truly over before he'd gone to her bed. That sleeping with Rebecca that one, last time had been nothing more than a moment of weakness. Of feeling guilty and sorry for the woman who'd made the mistake of marrying him.

That anger had helped a lot in those months of Rebecca's pregnancy when he had been struggling with having had to end things with Megan before they could even get started properly.

And then his world had collapsed around him. Rebecca had died and he'd been left with two tiny, fragile babies and he'd been facing the impossible.

And what had Megan done?

Walked out and gone to the other side of the world.

She hadn't even gone to the funeral.

No. Josh couldn't think of a way to change the subject. All he could do was sit there and stare at Megan.

She had found someone *else*?

Thank God Anna chose that moment to arrive at Josh's house to collect Crash.

They could both hear the front door opening and closing again. And Anna's cheerful call.

'It's only me. Anyone downstairs?'

Even though she was avoiding eye contact, Megan could feel the way Josh had been staring at her. As though he was shocked that she could have moved on with her life?

What the hell had he expected her to do? Sit and watch him raise Rebecca's children and pine for what might have been?

'In the kitchen, Anna.' Megan grabbed her coffee mug and pushed her chair back. She should have left Josh's house long ago. She shouldn't have come in the first place. Right now, she couldn't remember what it was she'd thought she was going to prove by doing so.

Whatever it had been, it felt like she had failed.

When she'd seen him gather Brenna into his arms and hold her like that. Pressing a kiss onto her soft, dark curls… The shaft of pain had felt like the knife that was permanently lodged in her heart had been twisted violently.

Their son had never known his father. Never had a cuddle or been kissed so lovingly. Stephen had never had a chance.

She and Josh had never had a chance.

And it was so…*unfair*.

'Gosh…' Anna breezed into the kitchen. 'It's raining cats and dogs out there now. Thanks for letting Crash inside.' She was grinning. 'Not that it's going to be easy dragging him away from your nice fire to go back to our cold cottage.'

'Want some coffee?' Josh sounded brusque. 'The kettle's still pretty hot.'

'No… My slow cooker is calling. I threw the makings of a beef stew in there this morning and it should be extremely well cooked by now.'

'It's been a long day,' Josh agreed. 'Did you get the chance to check on Mum again?'

'Of course.' Anna's smile was relaxed. 'She's fine, Josh. No pain and her rhythm's back to normal. I told her she's going to end up being in far better health from now on. Give her a week or two and she won't know herself. Oh, and I saw Ben in the car park. He said to tell you that ED's covered for the next couple of days. He's not expecting to see you anywhere near St Piran's unless you're coming in to visit your mum.'

'Thanks. I'll certainly need to be at home tomorrow. I'll have to sort out some extra childcare arrangements to take the pressure off Mum for a while.'

Megan had already rinsed out her mug but she did it again to avoid turning around and becoming a part of this conversation. Just because she'd stepped into the breach today it didn't mean she wanted to continue spending time with Josh's children.

In fact, she really *didn't* want to spend any more time with them. Or with him.

'I'd better be going,' she said brightly. 'And let you both get on with having your dinners.'

'I can drop you home,' Anna offered.

'No… I'll call a taxi.'

'Don't be daft. It's only a few minutes down the road to your cottage. You'll be waiting ages for a taxi in this weather.'

'I'm not staying at my cottage.'

'Why not?' Josh was frowning. 'Oh...you said it was uninhabitable, didn't you? How bad is it?'

'Pretty bad. Some pipes burst and the place got flooded months ago. The tenants moved out and left all their rubbish behind. There's no power. Probably no water either, except for what's still leaking out of the pipes.'

'Good grief...' Anna looked horrified. 'No wonder you can't stay there. Have you found somewhere in the village? I can drop you there.'

'I...um...haven't found anywhere yet. I was on my way to do that when I met Claire at the beach.'

'So it's my fault you haven't found somewhere to stay.' Josh was pushing his fingers through his hair in a gesture that Megan remembered all too well. 'You can stay here. We've got plenty of room.'

Megan could feel her jaw dropping. Stay under the same roof as Josh for a whole night for the first time in her life? Wake up and have breakfast with him? And his children? Why was fate throwing this stuff at her? Just how far did she have to go to prove she had moved on from Josh?

'Don't be silly.' It was Anna who spoke. Not that she could have read any of Megan's thoughts from her expression because she had moved to the door to summon Crash. She turned back to Megan with a smile. 'It's perfect timing. I'll be lonely while Luke's away and our spare room is all set up.' Her smile widened. 'Do you like beef stew?'

'I...ah...' Megan was shaking her head. Anna's cottage was just down the road. Next door to Josh. It was still too close for comfort.

'Just for tonight,' Anna said persuasively. 'You can sort out something else if you want to tomorrow, when it's not dark and raining. You look exhausted, Megan.'

She was. Emotionally as well as physically.

Just for one night? That's all it would need to be, wasn't it? She might even decide to sell up and be leaving all of this behind her by tomorrow.

'And it'll give us a chance to catch up.' Anna was looking wistful now. 'I've missed having you around, Megan.'

The persuasion was working. Megan felt far too weary to make any further protest. And she would enjoy Anna's company. The company of female friends was something she had missed badly after leaving here.

'OK,' she agreed. 'Just for tonight. Thanks, Anna.'

'Hooray...' Anna threw her arms around Megan and hugged her. 'It's so good to see you again.' She stepped back, still beaming. 'Isn't it, Josh?'

Megan didn't turn her head to see what reaction Anna's assumption that Josh was happy to see her had provoked but she got an inkling by the curiously raw note in his voice.

'Yes... It is.'

What else could he have said?

No, it was excruciatingly painful to see Megan again.

He'd thought he had it all finally sorted and now he was feeling like his perfectly ordered world had big cracks in it.

He would have preferred to never have laid eyes on her again.

But he couldn't have said any of those things in front of Megan. And they weren't even true. Not the one about preferring to never see her again, anyway. It might have been easier, certainly, but he would have always wondered where she was. How she was. Who she was with.

In the wake of both women and Crash leaving the house, Josh ransacked the fridge for enough leftovers to make himself a meal. He thought enviously of the hot beef stew Anna and Megan would be eating by now. Or was he more envious of Anna having the opportunity to find out more about Megan than she would ever be prepared to tell him? What would they be talking about?

That new *special* person in Megan's life? The one she was prepared to risk her life for by going back to Africa?

It should be *him*.

The thought came from nowhere and hit Josh like a sledgehammer. It wasn't framed as a regret. Or any kind of desire.

It was just there. A statement of fact. *He* was the person Megan should be with if she was going to be with anyone. Always had been. Always would be.

How could she get past that so easily?

Because it wasn't true for her? Maybe it never

had been. She'd found it easy enough to condemn him for sleeping with Rebecca, hadn't she? She'd never shown the slightest sign of forgiving him. Not even when he'd found himself at the most harrowing point of his life as a single father with premature twins.

At least his mother had been there for him. She had provided the glue that had let him stick his shattered life back together. It might present a very different picture from what he had imagined would be his future but...dammit...it was a good life.

Good enough, that was for sure. Better than most people had. He had a brilliant job. A wonderful home. His mother reminded him regularly how lucky they all were. How different it was from the cramped flat in London where she'd tried to raise him and his siblings after his father had finally walked out on them all for good. He was so lucky to have his mum here to help, too. Family. And he had two amazing children who were more important than anything else could ever be.

Including Megan?

Yes. Josh shoved his plateful of food into the microwave and set it to heat.

He'd made that decision long ago. The moment he'd known he was going to become a father. When he'd vowed not to be like his own father. He was well on the way to honouring that vow now. He couldn't—*wouldn't*—let anything undermine that.

Maybe he needed to take a new vow now. Not to be like his own mother. To try again and again in the name of love, only to be hurt beyond anything remotely acceptable. Because it wouldn't only be him who got hurt now, would it? It could be his children. His mother even. And that would turn him into his father again. God…life could be a complicated business sometimes.

A new vow wasn't really needed, was it? He could stick to the original one and he'd been successful so far.

Josh turned away from watching the plate go round and round inside the microwave. He had time to ring the coronary care unit at St Piran's and check on how his mother was doing. The sooner life got back to normal for them all, the better.

As if to underline the resolution, a faint cry came from upstairs. One of the twins had woken and needed comfort.

Josh left the kitchen.

'I'm coming,' he called. 'It's OK, darling. Daddy's here.'

Where he needed to be. Where he *wanted* to be. You could only live in the present, couldn't you?

You had to trust that the future would turn out all right.

And you had to let go of the past.

CHAPTER FOUR

PALE SUNLIGHT WAS filtering through the curtains in Megan's room when she woke up the next morning from one of the best sleeps she'd had for a very long time.

Perhaps the red wine she had shared with Anna over the meal of beef stew and crusty bread could take the credit. Or maybe it was the cathartic effect of having a heart-to-heart conversation with another woman, including more than a few tears being shed. The lullaby of the sound of surf had probably had a calming influence as well.

Whatever the reason, Megan was astonished by how good she felt as she luxuriated in that boneless relaxation of waking slowly from a very deep sleep, stretching cautiously and revelling in the fact that her joints were not giving even the slightest twinge. And then it occurred to her that it was November in Cornwall and for the sun to be high enough to be coming in her window meant that it had to be—

Good grief…ten a.m.?

Discarding the borrowed nightwear, Megan dressed in yesterday's clothes and hurried out of the room, although she knew Anna must have left for work long ago. Sure enough, there was a note propped up on the kitchen table with a set of keys beside it.

Wanted to let you sleep as long as possible. Help yourself to breakfast. There's cereal, toast and eggs around.

I got a ride to work so here are my car keys. You can drop them in to me later which will give everybody else a chance to say hi ☺
Love, Anna.
PS—you're more than welcome to stay again tonight. Your turn to cook?
PPS—enjoy the sun while it lasts!

Crash was nowhere to be seen. Back at day care at the O'Haras'? Thank goodness Anna hadn't asked her to drop him off. Megan didn't think she was ready to see Josh again yet. Maybe she never would be.

He had the perfect life. A job he loved. A fabulous home. Family around him. His mother and…and his *children*.

Megan had none of those things right now.

But…she did have plans, didn't she? She needed to hang onto that and decide what the next step should be.

Mulling over her options while she had a cup of coffee and toast didn't make things any clearer. Washing up her dishes, Megan looked out towards the little bay over the road from the Davenports' cottage. The surf still looked pretty wild but the clouds were white and billowing today, moving fast enough for the sun to make frequent appearances.

Getting a little bit of exercise and a blast of fresh, sea air was irresistible. Megan put her warm coat and gloves on and borrowed one of Anna's woolly hats to keep her hair from driving her crazy.

Gusts of wind strong enough to douse her with salt spray and almost knock her off her feet made it a struggle to walk in one direction on the beach but when Megan reached the end of the bay and turned around, it suddenly felt like she was flying. She held her arms out wide and laughed aloud from the childlike joy of it.

Seagulls were swirling overhead, riding the strong air currents, and they sounded as if they were shrieking from the excitement of it all. Megan didn't shriek but she was still laughing by the time she got back to her starting point and she'd never felt more alive. As if her blood was actually fizzing in her veins. She had to stop for a minute then to catch her breath and she looked up and down the bay, hugging herself with both arms.

She loved it here. So much.

The buffeting in the cold air and the fresh, sticky feel of salt spray she could taste on her lips had done more than restore her zest for life. It seemed to have had a cleansing effect as well. Not that Megan could have said exactly what had been blown away.

Maybe the disappointment of finding the home of her heart virtually derelict.

The backwash of the emotional disturbance that seeing Josh again had caused.

Or maybe doubts about the big decisions she needed to make about her future.

Whatever it was, right now it had gone and Megan was left feeling at peace.

At home.

She couldn't deny the sense of belonging to this little corner of the world. Could she really turn her back and walk away for ever?

It would be an easy way out, that was certain. But would she always miss it? Be haunted, as Charles warned her might happen, by thinking she had left unfinished business behind?

Worse than that, now that she'd seen the cottage, would she be left thinking she had dishonoured the memory of her grandmother—the woman who'd always been there for her? Who'd taken a frightened four-year-old and guided her towards adulthood with infinite wisdom and warmth?

'What should I do, Gran?'

The only sound in the wake of her plea for advice was the crash of the surf. Even the seagulls were silent for a moment. Megan took a last, deep gulp of salty air before turning to leave the beach.

She couldn't leave. Not yet, anyway. The sustaining memories held in this place were bigger than the heart-breaking ones. It was a sanctuary she couldn't afford to throw away if there was another answer. And she owed it to Gran to fix up the cottage as much as she could before she made any final decision.

Resolutely, Megan began walking back to Anna's cottage, wrapping her coat around her body to keep warm and sticking her hands in her pockets to keep the wind from sneaking into any gaps.

Even through the woollen gloves, she could feel something in her pocket. A small, hard object. She remembered what it was as she pulled it out. Claire's chain, which had caught on her scarf and broken yesterday. It was only now that Megan registered what was hanging on the thin silver chain. A tiny, silver shamrock.

Very Irish, she thought with a smile. And probably treasured. Was Claire fretting about losing it? She could take it in when she returned Anna's car keys. On the way, she could sort out a rental car for herself and find some tradesmen to come and start urgent work on her cottage.

* * *

By mid-afternoon, with the sun already taking a bow for the day, Megan pulled into the doctors' car parking area at St Piran's feeling weary but satisfied with her day.

She sat in Anna's car for a minute after turning off the engine. Just because she could. Because today was so different from yesterday and she could take her time. Because that awful stress of being afraid of what she would find here was gone.

Megan knew that Claire was going to be fine. She would probably have a new lease on life now and be healthier than she'd been in a long while.

She knew that she didn't have to imagine what it would be like to see Josh again. To wonder if her feelings would be strong enough to turn her carefully reconstructed world upside down. To be afraid that he might actually hate her for walking out of his life when he'd badly needed his friends.

And, as it was with the cottage, she could accept that this hospital was an important part of her personal history. That it held a lot of memories worth treasuring and that avoiding it was not only immature but it could lead to regrets.

Locking the car, Megan walked towards the sprawling, modern structure that housed a renowned medical facility. A helicopter was approaching, hovering just before coming down on the heli-pad. Such a familiar sound here because the A and E department had the reputation of being able to handle anything and it was the first choice in the area for any major trauma.

Thanks to Josh.

Children were also brought here rather than to other hospitals within easy flight distance because the paediatric department was equally first rate. They had the facilities, equipment and dedicated staff to cope with any traumatic or medical emergencies.

It was so familiar.

And so different from what Megan had been forced to get used to in a developing country that had far too little available in the way of facilities, even basic equipment and supplies, and far too few staff. It had been so easy to feel that she was making an important contribution there but was saving a little life in Africa any less satisfying than saving one here?

No. Parents were parents the world over and they all loved their children. It was just...different. The challenges were different and often unbearably frustrating because it could be purely luck that made something available there that would be taken totally for granted here, like an incubator or even antibiotics.

There were familiar faces to be seen on her way to the cardiology ward, including one of the midwives Megan had known well.

'Brianna...hi.'

'Megan...I heard you were back in town. How are you?'

'I'm fine. And you? Obviously back at work?'

'Only part time. The twins are setting new heights in being "terrible twos".' But Brianna was smiling, clearly loving motherhood.

Twins. There was something in the air around here. Reminders of Josh around every corner? Megan could feel herself trying to pull a protective layer around her heart. Putting up some 'road closed' signs.

Brianna was still smiling. 'I've got to run.

Home call to make to a new mother. But I'd love to catch up. Are you back for good?'

Megan shook her head with more emphasis than necessary.

'Oh, shame. We could sure use you. Did you know there's a consultant paediatric position being advertised as we speak?'

Again Megan shook her head. She hadn't known. Didn't really *want* to know, in fact.

'I'm just visiting,' she said, forcing a smile. 'But we should definitely have a coffee or something.'

Just visiting. The words echoed in her head after she'd said goodbye to Brianna. They felt wrong, somehow.

Did she still belong here, in the same way that part of her would always belong to Penhally? Did she belong in Africa now, where part of her heart would always be? Or maybe she needed to be somewhere that she had belonged to long ago. London.

Megan didn't know and it was a disturbing feeling. As if she was drifting.

Lost.

At least the map to the cardiology ward was

well remembered and easy to follow. Megan found Claire sitting up in bed, reading a magazine.

'Oh, my dear…' Claire's smile lit up her face. 'I'm so pleased to see you. I don't know how I'm going to thank you. Josh tells me you probably saved my life.'

The heartfelt gratitude was embarrassing but it was impossible not to return such a warm smile.

'I've got something else you might be pleased to see.' Megan fished in her pocket. 'The chain was broken but I had it fixed for you today when I was in Penhally.'

'My chain…' Claire took it from Megan almost reverently. 'Oh…'

'It looked like it might be special.'

Claire nodded, her face misty. 'My Joshie gave it to me for Mother's Day. He bought it with the first money he earned from his paper round. I think he was about six or seven.' Claire pressed the hand holding the chain to her heart. Her smile was rather wobbly now. 'Sorry,' she sniffed. 'It's all a bit…'

'Emotional. I know.' Megan's smile was sympathetic. 'You've been through rather a lot in the last twenty-four hours. I understand completely.'

More than Claire would know, in fact. Megan had been on a bit of a roller-coaster herself. She watched as the older woman's fingers trembled, trying to open the catch on the chain.

'Can I help?' She took the chain and Claire bent her head forward so that she could fasten it behind her neck. When she leaned back on her pillow her face was disconcertingly close. Those blue eyes so familiar.

'Thank you, lovie. Please…sit down for a minute. Have you got the time?'

'Of course.' Megan took off her coat and perched on the edge of the chair beside Claire's bed. She couldn't help casting her eye over the monitor still recording an ECG and up at the IV pole, where the bag of fluids was empty. Did she still need a line in and fluids running to keep a vein open in case of emergency?

'You're looking good,' she told Claire. 'Are the doctors happy with you?'

Claire nodded. 'I'm allowed to go home tomorrow as long as I behave myself today. They're going to do a…an echo-something-or-other in the morning.'

'An echocardiogram?'

'That's it. They did tell me what it would show but it all sounded very technical.'

'It gives them a way of looking at your heart and seeing how well it's pumping. They can measure the blood that comes out with every beat and give it a number. It's a percentage of the blood that was in that part of the heart. They call it an ejection fraction.'

Good grief…Megan knew she was hiding behind professionalism here. Avoiding talking about anything too personal because this was Josh's mother. The grandmother of Rebecca's children.

Claire seemed to see straight through her. She leaned forward and patted Megan's arm.

'I'm so glad you've come back,' she said softly. 'Josh will be too.'

But she hadn't come back. Megan opened her mouth to reiterate her visitor status but Claire was nodding.

'You're a star,' she told Megan. 'I saw your picture. In that refugee camp. You were holding a dear little baby and there were so many children all around you.'

Megan's eyes widened. 'Where on earth did you see that?'

'In that newsletter thing that comes from the organisation you work for. What's it called again?'

'Medécins Sans Frontières,' Megan said faintly. 'The MSF. Doctors without borders.'

'So it is.' Claire's gaze was oddly direct. 'Josh gets it delivered every month.'

'I…ah…' Megan had no words. Josh had been following where she was and what she'd been doing for the last two years? That was…unexpected. Flattering? Confusing, that was for sure.

'He needs things to keep him interested.' Claire's tone was almost offhand. 'Poor man, all he's got in his life are the children and his work. It's not enough, is it?'

Megan could only stare at Claire, her jaw still slack. What was Claire trying to say?

She didn't have to wonder for more than a heartbeat.

'He'd never admit it for the world.' Claire's

voice was no more than a whisper. 'But he's lonely, so he is.'

Megan took in a slow breath and tightened her jaw. Lonely? With two gorgeous children and his mum living with him? With his job and all his colleagues? His *perfect* life?

He was *lonely*?

And she was supposed to care about that?

For heaven's sake, Josh O'Hara didn't have to be lonely if he didn't want to be. He could have any woman he wanted. Back when she'd first met him, when he'd been no more than a talented but very junior doctor, he'd had the reputation of being a notorious womaniser. He'd been a legend. To have him even noticing the naïve bookworm of a final-year med student that Megan had been at the time, let alone focusing his well-deserved legendary skills in the bedroom on her for a whole night, had been unbelievable. When he'd been back with his ultra-cool friends days later and had ignored her, she'd known exactly how easily replaceable she'd been.

So what had changed? He was still impossibly good looking. In that unfair way men were capable of, he was only getting more attractive as he got older. He was still supremely confident, with good reason, given the accolades the emergency department of St Piran's Hospital regularly garnered. He was a prime example of pure alpha male and Megan could be absolutely sure that no woman in her right mind could be immune to the lethal Irish charm with which he could capture anybody he fancied.

So, if he *was* lonely for feminine company, why wasn't he doing something about it?

And why did the mere thought of him being lonely echo in her own heart like this?

Because, despite the new directions in which she had taken her life, she was lonely too?

Did she really think she could move on and find a way to ignore the person-shaped hole in her life that would never be filled?

There was no point in allowing that train of thought. If Josh was lonely, it had nothing to do with her. She couldn't allow it to. With a huge effort Megan focused on what was right in front of her.

An IV line that had blood backing up its length because the bag of fluids was completely empty and exerting a vacuum effect. She reached out and pushed the call bell.

'You need your IV sorted,' she told Claire. 'And I should really be getting going.'

It wasn't a nurse who answered the call bell. It was Anna.

'Hey…' She grinned at Megan. 'You called?'

'Hardly needs a consultant cardiac surgeon to remove a cannula or hang some more fluids but this is good. Saves me having to page you to give you your car keys.'

'How did you get on? Was it useful?' Anna glanced at the IV tubing taped to Claire's arm.

'Enormously. Thank you so much. I zipped all round Penhally and sorted out some contractors to start work on the cottage. They're charging like wounded bulls but the plumber and electrician both said they could start tomorrow.'

'Fantastic.' Anna was eyeing the monitor beside Claire's bed. 'It's all looking great,' she told her patient, 'but I'd rather keep your IV in for a bit longer. Think of it as an insurance policy against any complications. If it's there, we won't need it. Now…where's the trolley? Ah, there it is…' She moved to the corner of the room but turned to look at Megan as she pulled open a drawer. 'If they're not starting till tomorrow, that means you won't be able to stay there yet.'

'Probably not for a few days, no.'

'So you'll stay and keep me company?'

'If you're sure…' Being so close to the beach was as much of a draw card as Anna's company. 'And, yes, I'd be delighted to cook tonight. I'm going to go and pick up my rental car now and will do some shopping.'

'Oh…' Claire had been following the conversation, looking from one younger woman to another and back as though following a tennis match. Now she was beaming. 'You'll be just down the road, then, lovie. You'll have to come and have a cuppa, so you will.'

Anna excused Megan having to respond. She'd come back with a new bag of saline from the trolley drawer but exclaimed in frustration when she went to hang it on the hook.

'It's past its expiry date. It shouldn't even be in the trolley. That really isn't good enough.' Discarding the bag, she went back for another one.

Megan's jaw dropped. 'You're not going to throw it out, are you?'

'Have to. It expired a month ago.'

'But that's such an arbitrary date. You can see it's all right.' Megan held the bag up to the light. 'No goldfish swimming around. This stuff lasts for ever. It's only salty water. We wouldn't hesitate to use it in Africa.'

'Plenty more where that came from.' Happy with the new bag, Anna was changing over the giving set, pushing the spike into the port on the bottom of the bag. 'And not only fluids. I'll bet there are hundreds of things like cannulas and syringes that have to be discarded at every stocktake because they've gone over the date. Hospital policy. Hey…maybe we should gather them all up and post them to Africa.'

'That's not a bad idea. In fact…' Megan felt a fizz of real excitement '…it's a *brilliant* idea. My clinic would be over the moon to get a crate of supplies like that.'

'We could do some fundraising, too.' Claire didn't want to be left out of the discussion. 'There's plenty of grannies like me in the district and we'd love a good cause to have a bake sale or something for.'

'Oh, I couldn't ask you to—'

Claire held up her hand in a stop sign. 'Don't you say another word, lovie. I've been lying here wondering how I was ever going to be able to thank you for saving my life and this is it. I can not only say thank you to you but we can do something for all those poor children in Africa at the same time. It's perfect.'

Perfect. There was that word again. Funny how it was starting to grate.

'Go and talk to Albert White,' Anna advised. 'You'll need the CEO's permission before you start gathering up the old stuff. I'll ask Luke who else you could talk too as well. You could fill dozens of crates if you got some other hospitals on board with the idea.'

If nothing else, the excuse of going to talk to Albert White took Megan away from Claire and her disturbing confidences about her son's state of happiness. It also stopped Megan worrying about the downside of staying longer at Anna's place with it being next door to the O'Haras. It was a godsend to have something other than herself or Josh to think about as she walked through the hospital corridors, and the more she thought about it, the better the idea seemed.

By the time she knocked on the CEO's office door, she was more excited about it than she could remember being about anything for a very long time.

The last thing Josh O'Hara expected to see when he emerged from the lift on his way to visit his mother was Megan Phillips shaking hands with Albert White.

'Josh...' Albert was positively beaming. 'I heard about your mother. I'm delighted to hear today that she's doing very well.'

'You and me, both.' But Josh was looking at Megan, who seemed to be avoiding his gaze. She looked oddly...nervous? What was going on?

'You're not working today, are you, Josh?' Albert continued. 'Didn't Ben tell me he had things covered in Emergency?'

'I'm just here for a visit.'

'All by yourself? Where are those little ankle-biters?'

'Being babysat by one of Mum's friends from her grandmothers' group. Only she's a great-grandmother. You remember Rita—the ward clerk in NICU who retired a while back?'

Albert's eyebrows rose. 'Who could forget?'

Josh snorted softly. 'I know. She's a much nicer person these days now that her feet don't hurt from too much standing. Her great-grandson, Colin, goes to the same playgroup mine do. They call it "afternoons with the oldies" or something similar. Anyway…'

'Yes, yes. Must get on. I'll leave Megan to tell you the good news.'

Josh stared after the CEO as he bustled away.

'Was he actually rubbing his hands together?' he murmured.

'Probably.' Megan was biting her bottom lip.

'And didn't I see you two shaking hands? It looked like you'd made some kind of a deal.'

'Mmm.' Megan was still avoiding direct eye contact.

Josh sighed inwardly. He had a feeling that whatever it was, it was going to make life a little more complicated for him.

Megan was eyeing the button to summon the lift. Josh leaned against the wall. She'd have to reach around him to get to the button.

'So…is it a big secret?'

Megan sighed audibly. 'No. And you'll find out soon enough, I suppose. Anna had this idea...'

He listened to the plan of collecting out-of-date supplies like IV gear and drugs and old equipment that was being replaced and donating them to Megan's clinic in Africa. He had to agree it was a brilliant idea but he was only half listening to the words coming out of Megan's mouth. What was even more riveting was the way her mouth was moving. The flicker of real passion he could hear in her voice and see in her eyes.

It had the effect, he thought, that holding a shot of whisky under the nose of a recovering alcoholic might have.

So tempting.

He actually had to fight the urge to put his finger against Megan's lips and stop the words. And then to cover her lips with his own and silence them for a very, very long time...

And then Josh realised that Megan had stopped talking. He tried to pull back her last words from the ether before they evaporated completely.

'I'm not quite sure what this has to do with my department.'

'Albert made me an offer I couldn't refuse.'

'Which was?'

'He'll donate everything suitable that St Piran's can spare. He'll contact his fellow CEOs from other hospitals in the district and get them to pitch in. He'll endorse a hospital fundraiser to cover the shipping costs.' Megan was biting her lip again. 'He'll even throw in a ticket so that I can travel with the load and make sure it gets to the right place.'

Josh shook his head in amazement. 'That's an amazing offer all right.' But he couldn't shake the image of Albert walking away rubbing his hands together as though he'd got the better end of the deal. 'What does Albert get out of it?'

'Me,' Megan said simply. 'I've agreed to work here for the next few weeks to get a big project off the ground. He needed a paediatric specialist to oversee it.'

Josh was grateful for the wall he was leaning on. Now he could understand exactly why Megan had looked nervous. She knew that he wouldn't like this.

'The project's the paediatric triage and observation suite to go into A and E, isn't it?'

It had been a pipe dream for such a long time.

The busy emergency department with all the sights and sounds and smells that went with major trauma and life-threatening medical problems was a terrifying place to bring young children, especially when they were sick and even more vulnerable. And often, admitting them to a ward was not necessary but they did need observation for a period of time because, if you had the slightest doubt, you couldn't afford to send them home. A dedicated, child-friendly space that still had the capability to deal with life or death situations would put his department even more securely amongst the best in the country.

'Mmm.' Megan finally looked up. 'I couldn't say no, Josh. I did try, I can assure you.'

Really?

Maybe she was doing this to punish him.

Seeing her again had disturbed his equilibrium markedly. Feeling her presence in his house and seeing her close to his children had made visible cracks in the foundations of his new life. Even when she wasn't there, he could feel the way it *had* been last night. It had haunted him all day. So much so that he'd accepted with alacrity Rita's offer to babysit. So that he could escape.

Not only to visit his mother but to find refuge in the other half of his life.

His work.

How could he handle knowing that he would see her here every day? For weeks?

Megan had found her new life. In Africa. She'd found someone *special*.

Did she want to rub his nose in that? To remind him, on a daily basis, just how much he'd messed up his own life?

It was then that Josh realised he'd been holding eye contact with Megan just a shade too long. That he'd been searching her face for confirmation. But what he saw was something quite different.

Anxiety.

Fear, almost.

Why was *she* afraid?

'I could try and talk to Albert again,' Megan said quietly. 'If it's a problem.'

Josh could feel his head moving. Not in assent. He was slowly shaking it from side to side in a negative response.

Because he knew why Megan was afraid. She didn't want to be working near him any more than he wanted her to be. Because she was un-sure about whether she could handle it.

And she could only be that unsure if she still felt the same way about him as she had before she'd walked away two years ago. Before he'd ended things to stay in his marriage and be the father he'd had to try and be for his children.

But he wasn't married any more, was he?

Was that going to make a difference? Could he afford to even think about letting it make a difference?

Josh had no answer to that internal query.

And maybe that was what he needed to find out. It might be the only way he could avoid being haunted for the rest of his life by what might have been with Megan Phillips.

He could talk to Albert himself but if the in-centive that had been offered had been mas-sive enough to swing the deal when Megan was clearly feeling vulnerable, how could he do any-thing that might wipe out the reward she wanted so badly? If she didn't have something like this to keep her here, she might leave again, and Josh knew that if she left on such a disappointing note he would never see her again.

Besides, the CEO knew what he was doing.

Megan was perfect for the task.

Josh was still shaking his head. He added the hint of a smile as he eased himself away from the wall and allowed Megan free access to the lift button and escape.

'It's not a problem,' he said decisively. 'We're lucky to have you on board. When are you going to start?'

'In a day or two. As soon as I've got the renovations on my cottage underway properly. Maybe Thursday?'

'Excellent.' Josh tried, not very successfully, to widen his smile. 'See you then, Megan.'

He walked away. He knew Megan would have pushed the button for the lift but he also knew that she wasn't watching for it to arrive.

She was watching him.

He could feel it as clearly as if it were her hands and not her gaze touching him.

CHAPTER FIVE

WHAT *HAD* SHE been thinking?

Megan was shredding salad vegetables with far more force than required as she groaned inwardly yet again.

'I must be crazy,' she said aloud.

'Hardly.' The voice came from her mobile phone, which she had on speaker mode, propped on the kitchen windowsill. 'It's not every day that you get such a generous donation. It'll make a huge difference to the clinic, you know that.'

'But it's not a donation, is it? I'm going to have to earn it. By working...with Josh. He'll be looking over my shoulder the whole time. This is *his* baby. He was talking about it years ago. Before I left.'

'What's really worrying you, Megan?' The male voice was kindly. 'Not being able to do the job justice, or having to work that closely with Josh?'

'I—I'm not sure. It's complicated.'

'Relationships always are. You've got some serious history with Josh, we both know that.'

'It's not just him, Charles. It's the cottage and the hospital and…and Gran. When I think of family, I think of this place. These people. It's… confusing.' She twisted the iceberg lettuce in her hands, dividing it into smaller and smaller pieces.

'Which is precisely why you need to take time to get your head around it all.'

'But maybe that's the wrong thing to do.' Megan was separating lettuce leaves now and pulling at them to break them up even further. 'Maybe I should just pack it all in and come to London. What's the weather like?'

'Cold and grey.' She could hear the smile in his voice. 'I'm sitting beside the fire. I think Mrs Benson's got some roast beef and Yorkshire pudding in the oven for my dinner.'

'Mmm…nice. We're having fish and salad.' Megan eyed the lettuce she'd shredded into minuscule pieces, the tomatoes that had been diced to within an inch of their lives. Cucumber that should be discs but was now tiny triangles. 'I'm not sure it was such a good idea after all.'

'It's healthy. I'm pleased that you're looking after yourself. Oh, there's the bell. I'd better go and present myself in the dining room. Talk to you soon, love. When are you going to start the job?'

'On Thursday. I'm meeting all the contractors at the cottage tomorrow to make a list of everything that needs doing.'

'Don't overdo things.'

'I won't.'

Having said goodbye, Megan scooped the sorry salad into a bowl and turned her attention to crumbing the fresh fish fillets she'd bought in St Piran.

It was all Claire O'Hara's fault, she decided.

Telling her that Josh was lonely.

No. It was her own fault, for remembering what Claire had said in that moment when she could have said no to Albert. When, having come up with his brilliant idea, he'd given her a very significant glance and asked if—given her…ahem…history with Josh—she thought they would be able to work together again.

She could have said no. She probably could have said no and still received permission to collect at least something to contribute to the clinic, but the lure of being able to make a really significant difference had been huge.

And when she thought about working with Josh, all that came into her head was Claire's voice.

But he's lonely, so he is.

Why had he told her that his life was so perfect? Was he trying to protect her in some way?

And why did it bother her so much if he *was* lonely?

Because she understood? Because the words resonated at such a very deep level in her own heart?

Because the kind of love that she and Josh shared would never, ever go away completely— on either side—and because they could never be together, there would always be that empty... lonely space inside.

The fact that they couldn't make it work was sad but it didn't mean that she didn't want Josh to be happy. To close off that lonely space and move on.

Did it?

Charles had been wise, Megan concluded, slipping the fish into the oven to bake. She had to face this head on and find out exactly what was going on in both her head and her heart. She'd promised Charles that she would do that before making those final, irrevocable decisions about her future.

When she was really sure of herself, she could make sure that Josh knew that she was stronger now. That she didn't need protection. That she'd moved on successfully and was on the way to making her life as perfect as possible, too.

Did they both need to believe that in order to finally let go?

'Did you order this, Megan?'

'What is it?'

The nurse, Gina, started unrolling a large, laminated poster. A line of text became visible. 'It's a paediatric resuscitation chart.'

'Oh…good. That's to go on the wall behind where the IV and airway supplies are going in the main resus area. There should be a paediatric Glasgow coma scale and a classification of shock chart coming as well.'

'OK.' But Gina looked curious as she unrolled

the chart a little further. 'Aren't doctors supposed to know all this stuff about weights and drug dosages and things off by heart?'

Megan nodded, looking up from where she was sorting packets of supplies. 'Think of it as an insurance policy,' she said. 'In an emergency situation, the more time you can save and the more accurate you can be, the better.'

Behind Gina, she could see Josh approaching. This new area of the emergency department, taken from part of the plaster room and a couple of offices, was still a mess a week after the transformation had begun. There were workmen installing ceiling tracks for X-ray equipment, putting pipes in for an oxygen supply, sorting lighting and electrical fittings for monitors and computers, and installing phone lines and the fixed furniture like the central nurses' station.

When this exciting project was finished, St Piran's would have a six-bed observation unit where babies and children could stay for up to twenty-four hours without needing admittance to the main ward. They would also have two resuscitation areas. A main one that would have everything needed for a life or death emergency and a second one so that they could cope with more than one serious case at a time. The division between the two areas could be folded back, if necessary, to allow access to the state-of-the-art gear that would be going into the main part.

The whole concept would be something that many hospitals would envy. Josh O'Hara would get the credit for its inception and execution. No doubt it would generate huge publicity and kudos and his already stellar career would skyrocket even further. If he was at all concerned about how the result would affect his own reputation, he wasn't showing it right now. Josh looked relaxed and confident. His shirtsleeves were rolled up and a stethoscope was dangled carelessly around his neck.

It was by no means the first time Josh had wandered out of the main department to see what was happening with the set-up of the new paediatric wing and, of course, Megan had been rattled by the close professional scrutiny that had so many deeply personal undertones but she was finally starting to relax.

The tone of their interaction had been put into place on the first day. This was Josh's territory.

The career half of his perfect life. He clearly had no idea that his mother had suggested it wasn't so perfect to Megan and he seemed determined to demonstrate how happy he was in his work.

He talked easily and passionately about the new project, happy to discuss any queries or ideas Megan put forward. He interacted with his colleagues in a totally relaxed manner but she was left in no doubt about the respect he was given as head of department. And she'd seen him, in passing, treating patients. On one occasion holding someone's hand to reassure them, on another leading a full resuscitation on a badly injured trauma victim.

Megan had taken her cue from Josh. She was here as a colleague in a professional capacity, nothing more. To her relief, it wasn't proving as hard as she'd expected. Nobody could know how aware she was of Josh's proximity. How she could hear his voice across the whole department, even when he was speaking quietly. How she could sense his approach when she wasn't expecting him or looking in the direction from which he was coming. Like she had when Gina had been showing her the poster.

Megan acknowledged his approach with a tiny tilt of her head but continued talking to Gina.

'There are so many variables with paediatric patients,' she said, pleased to hear her voice sounding so steady despite the awareness of Josh infiltrating every cell of her body. 'And size and weight can make a critical difference to what size ET tube you might want to grab or, say, how much diazepam you want to give to treat a seizure.'

Josh was smiling as he stepped closer to Gina. He took the chart and unfurled it completely, holding it up against a wall to admire it. The movement made the muscles of his shoulders move under his shirt and the light caught the dusting of dark hair on his arms but Megan's attention was caught by his hands. Watching those long, clever fingers as they traced the different text boxes on the colourful chart.

'You can't weigh a sick baby or toddler easily,' he was telling Gina, 'but you can measure their length. Look…' He pointed to one side of a graph. 'I've got a two-year-old who's come in in status epilepticus and I want to give him an initial dose of IV diazepam. Here's his age. A quick measure shows me he's quite big for his age at just over a hundred centimetres so he's close to twenty kilograms, and I can double-check the dose I want to give him here...' Josh's hand made a rapid swoop towards a new box containing drug dosage information. Something in Megan's stomach mirrored the swoop.

'Cool.' But Gina was looking at Josh, not the chart, and the hero-worship was all too obvious.

She was young, Megan noted. And very pretty. It was also quite obvious that Josh had no need to be lonely if he didn't want to be. Not physically, anyway. Something much less pleasant than the previous sensation settled in her stomach. Deliberately, she dragged her gaze downwards and stared at the package in her hand. An ET tube. Cuffed. Smallest size.

'Want me to stick the poster up now?' Gina asked.

'No.' Megan's tone was a lot crisper than she'd intended. She smiled at Gina to disguise her inward turbulence. 'Put it on one of the trolleys in the corner of the observation room. I've got the mural painter in Resus at the moment, checking out how she can work around the fittings that are going in.'

'Mural?' Josh was finally looking at Megan directly as Gina moved away. She could feel it. 'In the resus room?'

She wanted to look up but resisted. Too hard to meet his gaze and still sound completely professional. So she reached for another handful of packages from the carton as though sorting ET tubes was too important a task to interrupt.

She risked a very quick glance upward, so as not to appear rude. 'Not as bright or complicated as the walls and ceiling in the observation area. I'm going for some leafy beanstalk plants with caterpillars on them and butterflies scattered over pale blue walls. A few on the ceiling too, where there's any space.'

'Sounds time consuming. I hope it won't put us behind on the target to have all the radiology gear installed by tomorrow.' She could hear the frown in Josh's voice. She could also feel the intensity of the look he was giving her go up a notch or two. But when she looked up, she found that he was watching her hands, not her face.

What was it about hands? She only had to let

her gaze rest on his, even if they were perfectly relaxed and just curled on the table in the staff-room or on his thigh when he was sitting down on the couch in there for once, and it always gave her that odd curl of sensation. The way it had when she'd been caught watching him trace the information on that resuscitation chart. Was it the memory of touch?

Did Josh get that by looking at *her* hands?

Megan sucked in a quick breath. 'It fits in with the overall philosophy of making this whole area as child friendly as possible,' she said evenly. 'You get conscious patients in Resus too, you know. Trauma victims, for example. If you can distract them from their pain and fear at all, it's going to help not only the assessment but it can potentially improve their status.'

It was quite true. Megan could almost hear Josh talking to the media about it when he was proudly showing off the new facility. Shock, from internal blood loss, he might say, is made worse by how fast the heart is beating. If you can calm a child down, you can slow the heart rate and potentially slow the rate of bleeding. People would lap it up. Everybody who contributed to the fundraising efforts would know that money hadn't been wasted in decoration for its own sake. Parents would feel happier knowing they could take their child into a place that went the extra mile.

Megan managed to smile as she looked up at Josh. 'I'll bet you could distract Brenna from something scary or sore by getting her interested in the big blue butterfly in the corner, or trying to find the yellow caterpillar with green spots on a leaf somewhere.'

The mention of his daughter did the trick. The intensity with which he'd been watching Megan faded rapidly and Josh relaxed. He even smiled back. A real smile that made the corners of his eyes crinkle.

Something crinkled inside Megan yet again.

Rebecca's daughter, she reminded herself, not only Josh's. The child that had been conceived when his marriage was supposed to be over.

'I take your point,' Josh conceded. 'A pretty resus room is commendable. What are you doing there?'

'Sorting airway supplies and deciding how we want to arrange them for ease of access. I'm thinking sets of the most commonly used sizes of ET tubes, cuffed and uncuffed, with guide wires but having appropriate LMAs and needle cricothyroidotomy kits with them as well to cover any complications.'

'Mmm.' Josh seemed to be listening intently and approving of what Megan was telling him.

Except that there was just a hint of a far-away gaze in his eyes. As though he was listening to her voice and thinking of something quite different. Had he remembered that it was her birthday today? Did he even know? And if he did, was that too far into personal territory to be allowable in this new phase of their relationship? Or should that be 'non-relationship'? Megan's train of thought became scrambled enough for her to sigh inwardly and grasp at something to ground her in reality again.

'How's Claire this week?'

'Doing really well, thanks.' Yes, she could see the way Josh blinked and refocused. 'Still getting tired easily but she's managing fine, thanks to her granny group friends. Oh...I had a message for you, in fact.'

'Oh?' Good grief... She was definitely losing

the ability to concentrate right now. Was that what Josh had been doing a moment ago? Being so aware of the sound of a voice that the words became almost meaningless?

Funny how you could feel a voice as much as hear it.

'They want to get involved in the Africa project. They're thinking of starting a toy drive. Mum asked if I could ask you to come and talk to her as soon as possible and tell her the kind of things they should be collecting.'

'Oh...' Megan bit her lip. 'That's very kind of them but, in general, toys wouldn't be the first priority. The really useful things might be exercise books and pencils and paper and crayons and picture books and...' Megan stopped, embarrassed. It was so easy to get carried away and start sounding over excited.

But Josh was smiling. 'That's what you need to tell mum and her cronies. I'm sure they'd be delighted to collect whatever would be most useful.'

'I'll do that. Thanks for passing on the message.' It might be an effort to turn away from that smile but Megan managed. She could even focus on the task at hand again. Out of the corner of her eye she saw Josh stare at her a moment longer but then he, too, turned away, rolling up the resuscitation chart as he let his gaze roam around what was happening away from this corner of the project.

The memories were all there, of course. And that powerful, indefinable pull between them, but it was all manageable. Under control.

It was, Megan mused, like looking at something magical. A tropical pool, maybe, on the hottest of days. Still and deep and so cool looking, surrounded by lush greenery. You knew that if you slipped into the water the sensation would be such bliss you might die from the sheer pleasure of it but you also knew that there were vicious piranhas circling beneath that smooth surface and the pain would be unbearable. The will to survive was enough to keep your feet on dry ground, no matter how uncomfortable or hard that might be.

Gina reappeared from the direction of the main department.

'Dr O'Hara? You're wanted. The condition of that little girl with asthma has deteriorated.'

'Coming.' Josh discarded the poster and began moving but his head turned. 'You've been given practising privileges here again, haven't you, Megan?'

Megan nodded. Albert White had made sure that it was legally covered. What's the use in having expertise like yours in the department, he'd said, if it couldn't be used if needed?

'Would you mind?' Josh was still moving but his head tilted in an invitation for her to follow him. 'She's on maximum therapy already and I thought we had it sorted. A second opinion would be welcome.'

'Sure.' Megan was on her feet and catching up. The thrill of anticipation was due to it having been so long since she'd faced a potential emergency with everything she might need at hand, she told herself.

It had nothing to do with the prospect of working side by side with Josh.

Six-year-old Bonnie was being given a continuous infusion of salbutamol but she was struggling to breathe. She could only manage sentences of one or two words in response to

Josh's questions and the outline of her ribs was visible even through the hospital gown due to the effort she was making to shift air.

'What's the oxygen saturation?' Megan queried, her hand on Bonnie's wrist, trying to count an extremely rapid heart rate.

'Down to eighty-six percent,' Josh told her. 'It's dropped. Respiration rate is up from forty to fifty-six.' He was frowning. 'Let's start a loading dose of aminophylline and get a chest X-ray to exclude a pneumothorax.' He raised his eyebrows at Megan, who nodded her agreement.

'We could start her on some positive pressure assisted ventilation, too.' She squeezed Bonnie's hand. 'We're going to change your face mask, sweetheart and give you one that's going to make it a bit easier for you to breathe. It's nothing to be scared about, OK?'

But Bonnie looked terrified. So did her mother, who was sitting close to the head of the bed, holding Bonnie's other hand. Megan moved closer to Josh and lowered her voice.

'We need an arterial blood gas. And we need to get her up to PICU as soon as she's stable.'

Josh murmured his agreement. He was still frowning. Somewhere behind them someone was shouting and a staff member was threatening to call Security if they didn't calm down. An X-ray technician bustled into the resus area and began moving equipment that clanked loudly against something else. An alarm was sounding on some monitoring equipment nearby.

Josh caught Megan's gaze. A gesture with his hand encompassed the undecorated walls with the array of potentially frightening supplies and machinery. 'The sooner we have our unit up and running, the better,' he muttered, 'don't you think?'

'Mmm.' Except it wasn't going to be *their* unit, was it? Megan was never going to work here again on a permanent basis. The realisation gave her a curiously sharp pang of regret.

She was working here right now, though, and over the next fifteen minutes her energies were directed solely to trying to help Josh stabilise Bonnie. Despite all their efforts, however, her condition was getting worse. Single-word responses became no responses at all and the child's level of consciousness was dropping noticeably. The level of oxygen in her blood, having gone up for a brief period, dropped with an alarming plunge. Her fingernails took on a bluish tinge.

'I'm going to intubate,' Josh decided. 'Rapid sequence. Megan, can you pre-oxygenate and then give me some cricoid pressure, please?'

Megan took her position and held the mask over Bonnie's face, turning up the flow of oxygen to try and get as much into her bloodstream as possible before any attempts to breathe were interrupted by the anaesthesia and intubation procedure.

She was ready to push on the front of the now unconscious Bonnie's throat to help Josh visualise the vocal cords and slip the tube into the correct position but his first attempt was unsuccessful. Megan could see the beads of sweat forming on his forehead. She reached above his head to silence an alarm on the monitor that was insistently beeping.

Josh looked up. He didn't have to say a word—the communication was simply there telepathically. If the next attempt was unsuccessful they would have to do something more invasive, like puncturing Bonnie's airway from the front of her neck. They couldn't afford to have her paralysed and not ventilated adequately for more than a few minutes. Megan had more experience with the smaller and sometimes difficult airways of children. She also had smaller hands that were capable of defter movement.

It wasn't anything like an admission of defeat on Josh's part to swap positions. He was simply taking the best advantage of the resources available.

The pressure of needing to perform to the best of her ability was countered by the knowledge that Josh had enough confidence in her to give her the chance. Megan didn't realise she was holding her own breath until she felt herself release it in a sigh of relief when the tube slipped into place and she could hear the air entry into Bonnie's lungs with her stethoscope as Josh squeezed the bag attached to her face mask.

The tension was still there for the next few minutes as they hooked Bonnie up to the ventilator and adjusted settings until they were happy with the way she was breathing and the amount of oxygen that was circulating in her bloodstream. And then Megan went with Bonnie to the paediatric intensive care unit to see her settled in and her care passed to the medical team on duty.

Finally, Megan returned to the main part of the emergency department because she wanted to tell Josh that the little girl appeared to be stable and she was already showing some signs of improving.

Josh was standing beside the triage desk, along with several nurses. He was holding a huge bunch of red roses wrapped in Cellophane. He didn't see Megan approaching because he was reading the small card stapled to the Cellophane.

Red roses. The most romantic of flowers. Who was the lucky recipient? Megan wondered. Or had someone sent them to Josh? Either way, she was experiencing a rush of emotion that was a long way from being pleasant.

Until Josh looked up and smiled at her.

'These are for you,' he said.

The unpleasant heaviness in her belly twisted

and tried to break up and form something entirely different. Except that Josh's smile wasn't reaching his eyes.

'Apparently, it's your birthday,' he added.

'Oh… Happy birthday, Megan.' The chorus came from several staff members but Megan barely heard them. If Josh was surprised to learn that it was her birthday today, it meant that the flowers couldn't possibly have come from him.

And that meant…

Josh had her pinned with his gaze. 'So, who's this Charles?' he asked, his tone deceptively casual.

This was it. A defining moment. There was a choice to be made. Did Megan stick to her new plans for her future or was she going to allow the past to hold her back?

Could she finally accept that what she had once wanted more than life itself was never going to happen and take the final step that would set Josh—and herself—free?

There really wasn't a choice to make, was there?

Megan took a deep breath and spoke into the waiting silence, ignoring all the expectant faces around her, except one. She was speaking to Josh here.

'Charles is my fiancé,' she said quietly.

CHAPTER SIX

Fiancé?

Megan had a fiancé?

He shouldn't feel this shocked, Josh realised. What had he expected—that Megan would stay single for the rest of her life because she couldn't marry *him*?

The chorus of 'happy birthdays' had turned into a round of congratulations. And questions. Who was Charles? Where had she met him? How long had they been engaged?

'He's a tropical diseases specialist,' he heard Megan telling them. 'I met him when he came out to Africa. He lives in London and…and we only got engaged very recently.'

'Is that why you're not wearing a ring?'

'Ah…yes…'

The hesitation was tiny. It might not have even been significant except for the way Megan's gaze finally moved to meet Josh's intent stare. The contact was brief but he registered two things. That there was more to this engagement than Megan was saying and that she was shocked by the way he was staring at her.

Fair enough. Josh pasted a smile on his face. Fortunately he had long since let go of that bunch of flowers.

'Congratulations, Megan,' he heard himself saying in a perfectly normal voice. 'I hope you'll be very happy. Now, you'll have to excuse me. I want to go and see how Bonnie's getting on.'

It was a good enough reason to walk out of the department, wasn't it? Josh hadn't banked on being followed, however. He increased his pace.

'Josh...wait...' Megan was closing the gap. 'That's what I came to tell you.'

'What?' He didn't turn his head. 'That you're *engaged*?'

'No...' The word was a sigh. 'That Bonnie's doing well. Tidal volume's increasing and her blood chemistry's improving. She's quite stable.'

'Good. I'd still like to see for myself.' Josh kept walking.

'Josh...' This time the word was a plea. 'Don't be like this...please...'

Her voice was quiet enough to carry no further than his own ears but two nurses coming towards him along the corridor were giving him frankly curious stares. And then they gave each other a significant glance. He could almost hear the newsflash that would hit the hospital grapevine in the very near future.

It's happening again. They can't even work together for five minutes without the sparks flying. What is it with the chemistry between those two?

No. It wasn't happening again. Or it wouldn't be if he could get a grip and stop behaving like a petulant teenager. He forced himself to slow down. To turn and give Megan a direct look.

'I need coffee,' he was saying as the nurses passed them. 'How 'bout you?'

He hadn't banked on the cafeteria being so deserted for once, any more than he had on Megan following him. They ended up sitting at one of the prized tables by the windows and there was nobody to overhear their conversation.

Megan had been very quiet during the walk to the cafeteria and while they fixed their drinks. Now she wasn't even tasting her coffee. She'd sat down at the end of the table, at a right angle to him, the way they'd been in his own kitchen. As though she didn't want the barrier of the table between them. Did she feel like he had? So close but not close enough?

'I'm sorry,' she said. 'I…should have told you about Charles the other night.'

Josh made a noncommittal sound. She had, hadn't she? When she'd talked about that 'someone special' still in Africa?

'It's…complicated,' Megan continued. 'I'd like to explain.'

Josh wasn't at all sure he wanted to hear anything more about Megan's engagement. He averted his gaze. 'Why? What's the point?'

The silence made him look back and the expression on Megan's face made him catch his breath. His question had made much more of a direct hit than he'd intended. She looked… stricken?

Why? Was she embarrassed at letting him know she'd found someone she loved more than him?

Ashamed that this was evidence that she'd found it easy to move on?

Or did she wish that things could have been different?

Megan's lips were moving. They trembled, which made the words sound shaky.

'I don't want you to hate me,' she whispered.

Josh could actually feel something melting inside him.

That anger at the way Megan had refused to believe him when he'd tried to explain how he'd ended up in Rebecca's bed that night. At the way she had walked out of his life at such a dark time when Rebecca had died. He could feel all the resentment he'd clung to just melting. Evaporating.

How could he ever hate the only person he had and ever would truly love?

He had chosen to end things between them. He'd pushed her out of his life so that he only had to think about being a good father and he'd had good reason to do that. The best reason because he'd known how dangerous it was to rely on having a love like that in your life. Having his mother alone and looking older than she should for her years was a reminder he could tap into every day, with the added bonus of remembering what that relationship had been like for himself and his siblings. How it was the children who could be hurt most.

He'd done the right thing. The only thing he could have done, anyway. He'd honoured his vow. But it didn't mean that he didn't want Megan to be happy, did it?

Of course it didn't.

'I don't hate you,' he said aloud. The smile he could feel tugging at his lips came from somewhere very deep. Very tender. It was just there. Kind of like the way his hand moved to cover one of Megan's. 'I could never hate you, Megan.'

He had to let go of her hand. But not quite yet. The warmth and silky feel of her skin was irresistible. His thumb moved over it. The memories of this hadn't done reality justice. He needed to capture it properly.

'Charles is...' Megan's voice sounded curiously thick, as though clogged by tears she was holding back. 'It's not perfect, you know...but... but what we had—it's gone, Josh—and I...I had to try and move on...'

'Of course you did.' The movement of his thumb had become something to comfort Megan now. 'I'm happy for you. Really, I am.'

'You'll move on, too.' He could actually hear Megan swallow.

'No.' Josh pulled his hand away.

It wasn't going to happen because the choice was unacceptable. He couldn't be with Megan because, even if he could somehow exorcise the ghosts of his own childhood, it was too late. She had found someone else. And to be with anyone else would be a shell of a marriage. The way it had been with Rebecca. He'd only end up messing with someone else's life and he'd vowed never to do that again.

'You still blame yourself, don't you? For everything.'

Josh said nothing.

This time it was Megan who, after a long and increasingly tense silence, reached out and caught his hand.

'It wasn't your fault,' she said softly but fiercely. 'I'm just as much to blame for getting pregnant that first time. And I didn't tell you. That was wrong. You thought it might be your son you were trying to save that night in Emergency but even then I didn't tell you. I let you wonder about that and be haunted for years and years. I…I'm sorry, Josh. I know it was a terrible thing and neither of us will ever forget but it's far in the past now. We need to let it go.'

'I married Rebecca,' Josh muttered. 'I can blame myself for making her life miserable.'

'She chose to marry you,' Megan said quietly. 'And, from what I heard, you'd made it very clear that you didn't want children. But you gave up what you *did* want, didn't you? For the children. For her.'

Josh had a lump that felt like it had sharp edges stuck in his throat. Oh, yes…he'd given up what he'd really wanted and it had felt like something was trying to die a slow and painful death inside him during those months when he'd pushed Megan away.

He couldn't tell her that, though, could he? Not when she had moved on and found someone else.

Except…she was still holding his hand. Really holding it now. Somehow their hands had moved and now their fingers were intertwined. Josh could feel himself being drawn closer. His head was moving. Something in Megan's eyes was pulling him closer and closer.

Any moment now and he would be close

enough to touch her lips with his own. In his peripheral vision Josh could see a group of staff coming into the cafeteria. If he kissed Megan right now, it would be all over St Piran's in a matter of minutes. And the worst thing was, he didn't give a damn.

Right up until the realisation hit him that this newsflash would come right on the heels of the news that Dr Phillips was engaged to some eminent specialist from London. Another relationship would be under threat. And it would be his fault.

History would be repeating itself.

Somehow, Josh found the strength to break that magnetic pull. To untangle their fingers and move himself away.

The group of nurses on early dinner break were heading for a table near theirs now.

'So…it's going well, isn't it?' Josh said, a little more loudly than he needed to. 'Our paediatric wing is going to be something for St Piran's to be proud of, don't you think?'

Megan knew instantly that Josh was trying to put them back onto a professional footing that wouldn't attract any more than mild curiosity from other staff.

It was a million miles away from the space they'd been in only seconds ago.

What exactly had happened there? She could have sworn that Josh had been thinking about *kissing* her.

And, dear Lord…all she had been able to think about was how much she wanted him to.

'Hey, Megan…' The midwife, Brianna, was amongst the group of nurses. She veered closer, a packet of sandwiches in one hand and a bottle of water in the other. 'I've been hearing great things about what's happening in A and E.'

'Yes, it's going really well, thanks.' Megan's smile included Josh. They could do this, it was intended to imply. They could put both their conversation and their interaction with each other back onto a purely professional footing.

Brianna was smiling at Josh. 'Is it true that a member of the royal family is going to come and cut the ribbon for the opening?'

'I believe so.' Josh's smile was as lazy and gorgeous as any Megan had ever seen. She could still see the lines of tension creasing the corners of his eyes, though. Could Brianna sense the undercurrents happening here?

Apparently not. 'How exciting,' she was saying to Josh. 'You'll be all over the news on telly. You're going to be *so* famous after this'

Josh's smile faded. 'I'm not interested in being famous,' he said. 'It's St Piran's I want to put on the map. And not because it has the flashest emergency department but because of the standard of care people get when they come through our doors.'

'Mmm…' But Brianna was grinning. 'Maybe we'll all be famous.' She turned back to Megan. 'You'll still be here, won't you? For the grand ceremony?'

'I expect so.' It was only a couple of weeks away, wasn't it? Megan hadn't made any plans to leave before then. In fact, she still hadn't made any definitive plans for what was coming next in her life. Decisions had to be made. Was she using this new project as a means of procrastinating? 'I've still got a lot of work to do on the cottage to get it back into shape.'

'I saw all the vans parked outside when I drove past yesterday,' Brianna nodded. 'Looks like you've got every tradesman in Penhally on the job.' She glanced down at the packet of sandwiches in her hand. 'Oh, help. I'd better eat or my break will be over. Nice seeing you again, Megan. You're looking a lot better than when you arrived. I think being home must be agreeing with you.'

Being home? Was that how everybody was seeing this visit?

If she was honest with herself, it was how it felt. Breathing in the sea air every morning. Working in a hospital that was as familiar to her as her own home. Being with people she knew so well. People she respected and liked.

Being close to Josh…

She couldn't really call it a comfort zone with the kind of undercurrents she'd been so aware of just a few minutes ago but she couldn't deny the attraction of the familiarity. The feeling of home. A huge part of who she was belonged here and it was going to be a terrible wrench when she left again.

Megan could feel Josh watching her.

'You're not living back in the cottage again, are you? With all that work still going on?'

She nodded. 'I felt a bit in the way after Luke got back from New Zealand. It's not so bad. I can navigate through all the ladders and paint pots. I have hot water and electricity again. I'm going to start on the garden this weekend.'

Oh…help. Should she tell Josh that Charles was planning a visit to come and help? But then she might feel obliged to tell him more about why they'd become engaged and that might lead to a conversation that would take her in the opposite direction from that she needed to go. Bridges might well get burned behind her if that happened and right now those bridges were an insurance policy.

This was the easiest way through it all, wasn't it? She was getting married to someone else and moving away and that would be an end to it all. For good.

But Josh was making a face that suggested even working in her garden was a bad idea.

'I was supposed to tell you,' he groaned. 'And Mum will have my guts for garters if you don't say yes.'

'About talking to her? The toy drive thing? I'll pop in after work.'

Josh shook his head. 'About Saturday. It's the twins' second birthday party. She's decided that you have to be the guest of honour.'

'Oh...I don't think that's...' A good idea? Of course it wasn't. It was a family occasion. A celebration of exactly why she and Josh could never be together.

It was a horrific idea, in fact. No way could she put herself through that.

Except that she made the mistake of meeting Josh's gaze and it was clear that he knew precisely how hard it would be. And not only for her.

'There's going to be lots of people there,' Josh told her quietly. 'And as far as Mum and everybody else is concerned, you saved the lives of Max and Brenna when they were born. Just before...before you left Penhally. And you saved the life of their grandmother virtually the minute you got back. They want to thank you and they've decided that the birthday party is the perfect venue. They'd be very disappointed if you couldn't come.'

Megan swallowed. Hard.

'You don't need to stay long. It's a lunchtime

party. You could just come for a cup of tea or something. Please?'

He cared so much, Megan realised. He didn't want his mother to be disappointed. He was quite prepared to do something that was probably going to be as difficult and uncomfortable for him as it would be for her, for the sake of someone else he cared about. How could she not be caught by that plea when that ability to care about others was one of the things she loved so much about this man?

'OK.' The word was a whisper. 'I'll come. I'll talk to Claire about what time and things when I see her later.'

The warmth of the smile Josh gave her stayed with Megan for some time. Well after they'd left the cafeteria and gone back to finish their day's work. The evidence of how Josh could put the needs of others over his own needs stayed alongside the memory of that smile and they were both on her mind as she drove home.

And then it happened. Not in a blinding flash but bit by bit. Random thoughts that came out of nowhere like pieces of a jigsaw puzzle and floated until she began slotting them into place. When the final picture came into view, it was enough of a revelation to make her pull off the road. Not that there was a patch of beach to walk on here but it was a parking area designed to let people appreciate the wilder parts of the Cornish coastline. Even in the dark, the white foam of the surf as it boiled over the rocks at the bottom of the cliff was spectacular and the sound of the sea loud enough to make coherent thought too hard.

The picture was still there, though.

Josh…unable to prevent himself from doing what someone else wanted him to do so badly.

A marriage that had been in tatters. A marriage that Josh had felt guilty about having embarked on in the first place simply because he'd been lonely.

A woman who had been bitterly disappointed in how it had turned out. Who had been obsessed by her need to have a baby.

Josh had said that she'd done it on purpose. Because she'd wanted a baby. It had been her way of trying to keep them together.

Had it been a desperate, last-ditch attempt

to save her marriage or to try and at least get pregnant?

Had Rebecca planned some kind of seduction and empowered it by playing on her husband's guilt? Megan remembered what Tasha had tried to tell her but she had been too desperately un-happy to listen. The marriage had been over for a long time, she'd said. Rebecca had probably been lying in wait on the bed in a skimpy set of underwear or something.

She'd been playing games.

Just this one more time…

How could Josh have been cruel enough to refuse? If he had, it wouldn't have been the ac-tion of a man who cared as much as she knew he was capable of caring.

It had only been that one time. Josh had told her that, too. A *mistake*, he'd said, and his voice had been agonised enough that she knew he'd been telling the truth.

And it had been weeks before he'd come to *her* bed that night. Had it been the final point of his marriage? One that had been definitive enough for Josh to know he had to leave it behind and move to where he really wanted to be?

How could *she* have been so judgmental?

She'd made it all about herself, hadn't she? She'd been so hurt by the idea that he'd slept with Rebecca even on a single occasion when they'd both been caught by the pull of the irresistible tide that had drawn them back together.

Megan had thrown up an impenetrable barrier right there, on the spot. A barrier that had made it unthinkable that she could ever be with this man she'd loved so much because he'd slept with his wife.

Once.

She'd seen the twins as evidence of his infidelity, for heaven's sake. Those gorgeous children who were the only children of his own Josh would ever have. Children he could never have had if he had been with her. They had his genes. His looks. His personality, probably, judging from the little she'd seen of them.

They were half-Josh. How could she not love them, if she let herself?

But she'd run away. Put thousands and thousands of miles between herself and those tiny babies. Between herself and Josh when he must have needed all the support he could get.

And right now, with tears coursing down her face, Megan could see it for what it had been.

A *mistake*.

They'd both made them. The difference was that Josh had known instantly about the mistake he'd made. It had taken two years and being forced to come home for her to recognise hers.

And the saddest thing of all was that there was nothing she could do about it. It was far too late. She'd run and she'd been away long enough for Josh to put his new life together. A life that he was determined to protect for the sake of the people he loved most.

His children.

A life that didn't—*couldn't*—include her.

CHAPTER SEVEN

A BIRTHDAY PARTY for two-year-olds was bound to be an emotional roller-coaster. Shrieks of delight and peals of laughter were punctuated by the odd bout of tears and even a tantrum or two.

Beneath a sea of balloons and streamers, the furniture in the O'Hara house had been pushed back to give more space both for the children to play and for the small crowd of accompanying adults to supervise as well as enjoy a social gathering of their own.

Claire's fellow grannies from the play group were there, including Rita who had brought her granddaughter Nicola Hallet and her great-grandson Colin. Brianna was there with her twin daughters Aisling and Rhianna. Anna and Luke had brought Crash.

'On request.' Anna laughed. 'But he's our fur child and he fits the age group.'

The look that passed between Anna and Luke

at that point had more than just Megan wondering if a less furry child was a not-so-distant prospect but there was no chance to ask her friend whether she was keeping a secret.

The party was full on. Timed for the middle of the day so that the young participants could go home for a sleep when it all got a bit much, there were gifts to open and games to play before the food was served.

Megan had offered to help in the kitchen where Claire and her friends were setting out tiny sandwiches cut into the shapes of animals and heating small pizza squares and chicken nuggets, but Claire shooed her back into the living area to have fun. On her way out of the kitchen Megan saw the dessert platters of bite-sized pieces of fresh fruit and two cakes. One a pink pony-shaped creation and the other an impressively green dinosaur with lurid, candy-covered chocolate buttons for spots. She was smiling as she joined the main gathering. Saving the bright food colouring for just before the toddlers were taken home was smart thinking.

Fun was the last thing Megan had expected to have when she'd steeled herself to follow up her promise to attend this party. She had spent the last few days in a state of confusion that had bordered on unbearable. Charles was driving down from London today and he had every right to expect that she would have achieved her purpose for staying on here by now. That she would have come to terms with her past and would be able to face her new future with confidence.

But, if anything, after the startling insight of how much she could blame herself for this whole, sad, star-crossed-lovers' story that she and Josh had created, it had only become harder to untangle the web of memories and emotions. It was much, much easier to let herself become distracted. To be drawn into the moment by concentrating on her work or the new project of collecting donations for the clinic or...amazingly... having *fun*.

Her trepidation had vanished only seconds after she'd walked in, carrying her gifts. It had evaporated the moment the twins had spotted her and come running.

'*Meggy.*'

That they'd been more interested in receiving cuddles than the brightly wrapped gifts was testament to how they were being brought up, Megan decided. She was the one to use the gifts as an excuse to call time from the tangle of warm little limbs wrapping themselves around her body.

Around her heart.

Josh was right there, a proud smile on his face, when his children remembered to say thank you for their gifts.

And then the children had wriggled back into the festivities and it was just Josh so close. Before Megan had had a chance to centre herself. She could still feel the overwhelming pull of those cuddles. The unconditional love…

'Great choice.' Josh was still smiling but there was a question in his eyes. 'Well done.'

Megan ducked her head. It was almost too much, receiving praise from Josh on top of the emotions his children had just stirred in her. And she didn't want to answer that question. The one about how she felt about these children. Maybe she didn't even want to think about it.

'The assistant in the toy shop has to get the credit,' she said. 'She told me that dress-ups were always a winner at this age.'

So now Max had a bright yellow Bob the Builder hard hat on, a tiny tool belt clipped around his waist and a miniature high-vis vest over his own clothes. And Brenna had pulled on the tutu skirt with the elasticised waist and put the sparkly tiara on her dark curls and was refusing to let go of her wand with the star on the top. She was waving it like a stern conductor as she danced to each burst of music for the game of musical cushions.

All the children followed her lead and were dancing with varying degrees of competence and balance. Josh's smile was as misty as those of any of the watching adults. He was actually forgetting to stop the music so that the children could make a dash for available cushions.

Megan found herself watching Josh instead of the game, knowing that her own smile was also coming from a very tender place in her heart.

Something had changed in the last few days.

Something very fundamental.

The anger had gone, hadn't it? That sense that Josh had betrayed her by sleeping with Rebecca.

And with it had gone the entire foundation on which she'd built her conviction that they could never be together. It seemed to have simply crumbled away.

Where did that leave her now?

Emotionally available?

Not really. There was Charles to consider now. And the pull of what she'd left behind in Africa.

Megan certainly couldn't forget about Africa. It seemed like it was the only thing people here wanted to talk to her about.

Wendy, the grandmother of three-year-old Shannon, couldn't wait to tell her about the bake sale planned for the next week.

'We're hoping to raise over a hundred pounds,' she told Megan. 'We're going to spend it at the bookshop.'

Margaret, who was at the party with two grandchildren, four-year-old Liam and his younger brother Jackson, overheard Wendy and rushed to join the conversation.

'Mr Prachett at the bookshop is giving us a great discount and he's found a line of picture books that have no text but still tell stories. And he's going to donate lots of pencils and paper, too.'

'The school's on board,' Wendy added. 'Every

child has been given an exercise book and they're decorating the covers in art class.'

Another granny, Miriam, offered Megan a cup of tea and a proud smile. 'I'm in charge of clothing donations,' she said. 'I've got two huge crates in my sewing room and I'm washing and mending and ironing everything before it gets packed. We're only accepting lightweight items like cotton dresses and shorts and T-shirts. Will that be all right, do you think?'

'I'm sure it'll be wonderful,' Megan responded. It was impossible not to be touched by the enthusiasm and generosity of these women. 'You're all wonderful. I can't believe how this project keeps growing and growing.'

'It's you who's wonderful,' Miriam said. 'We're having fun collecting things but we're still in our own comfort zones, aren't we? With our families safe and healthy around us. You're the one who was prepared to go to the end of the earth to really help.'

Josh was supervising a bubble-blowing contest but was standing close enough to overhear Miriam's words. When he looked towards them, his glance had none of the admiration of the women around her.

'Megan's an angel,' he said crisply. 'Just ask my mother.'

The tone was light enough to make the people around her smile. Maybe it was only Megan who could hear that the words covered something painful. They both knew the real reasons for her heading to Africa two years ago and it hadn't been entirely altruistic, had it?

Would she do it again, knowing what she knew now?

Fortunately, Josh had turned back to the bubble blowing and there were much easier questions to answer.

'What's it like?' Wendy asked. 'In the camp?'

Megan deliberately censored the first impressions that always came to mind. The unbearable heat and filth. The suffering of so many people. 'Huge. Like a fair-sized city, really, with a hundred and thirty thousand people in the camp and another thirty thousand or so around the edges.'

'It can't be an easy place to live.'

Megan shook her head. 'No. It's hot and dirty and there are pockets of violence but it's the disease that's the worst of it. There are probably eight thousand children suffering from malnutrition and so many orphans who lose their parents to things like AIDS. And then there are other diseases like dysentery and malaria and dengue fever to cope with.' She deliberately stopped herself going any further. A birthday celebration was no place to be telling things like they really were. She could do that somewhere else. At one of the fundraising events, maybe.

But the older women were hanging on every word. They tutted in sympathy.

'And the clinic? Is it like a medical centre or a proper hospital? Do you have operating theatres and maternity wards and things?'

'Oh, yes…it's a proper hospital but very different from St Piran's, of course. And we struggle to cope with what we have to work with.'

Megan's attention was caught by what was happening behind Margaret. Brenna was having trouble with her bubbles because she wasn't holding the loop anywhere near her mouth when she was blowing. Josh was crouched beside her. He closed her little fist over the handle of the loop and dipped it into the soapy water and then held it up in front of her mouth. She could see him miming what she needed to do with her lips and breath.

Brenna sucked in a big breath and whooshed it out and a stream of small bubbles exploded into the air. Her face lit up with a grin that went from ear to ear and Megan could see the way Josh's eyes crinkled as he grinned back. Even if she hadn't been able to read the love he had for his daughter on his face like that, she would have been able to feel the glow of it.

'Sorry, what was that?' She'd completely missed something Wendy had been saying.

'I read in the paper that other hospitals are joining St Piran's to donate old equipment and drugs and things. Isn't that marvellous?'

'It certainly is.'

'Dengue fever.' Miriam was frowning thought-fully. 'That's what you got sick with, wasn't it?'

'I'm much better now.'

'You look it. Must be the lovely sea air around here that's done the trick.'

'Mmm…' But Megan was having trouble focusing on her health or anything else right now. She was still watching Josh and remembering another time when she had read that kind of infinite love on his face. Way before Brenna had been born. Before he'd even known she was a possibility.

That love, seen in the half-light of that on-call room, had been purely for *her*.

And Josh would have seen the mirror image of it on her own face.

She could feel the glow of it all over again. So much so she needed to take off the cherry-red cardigan she had on over the soft white shirt she had teamed with her jeans. Had Josh sensed something of what she was thinking? Was that why he was suddenly there, his hand extended?

'Let me take that for you. I can hang it up with the coats.'

'Yes…' Wendy was nodding with satisfaction. 'You've got a nice bit of colour in your cheeks now, dear.'

Megan could certainly feel that colour, which must have heightened as Josh's hand brushed hers in relieving her of the cardigan. Feeling flustered, she avoided meeting his gaze, but that didn't help because she found herself looking at his hand. Holding an item of her clothing.

Oh, help... She had to excuse herself.

'I might see if your mum needs some help in the kitchen,' she muttered.

'See?' Josh had raised an eyebrow. His lazy grin was charming every female within range. 'I told you she was an angel. You could just enjoy yourself, Megan. You don't have to work, you know.'

Megan shook her head with a smile. It must be time to serve the party food and it was just too disturbing, being this close to Josh and re-membering things like that moment in the on-call room. *Feeling* things like the way that had made her feel.

Something huge had certainly changed but was it only on her side?

She was only half the equation here.

Josh had built his own foundation to anchor the barrier of them ever being together. The con-crete had been poured the day he'd come to tell her that Rebecca was pregnant. Megan had prob-ably added some steel reinforcing rods herself when she'd walked out without even having the courtesy of attending Rebecca's funeral.

He must have been so hurt by that. The subtle

edge to that "angel" comment he'd made suggested that it hadn't been buried far below the surface. And maybe it had just added to the anger simmering in the wake of her accusation that he'd been lying about his marriage being over. That he'd treated her like a bit on the side.

Could he ever forgive her for that?

He'd said he didn't hate her.

That he could *never* hate her.

And, when he'd said that, he'd looked…as if he'd wanted nothing more than to close the gap between them and kiss her senseless.

There was still something there between them, that much was obvious.

A big something.

But was it big enough? Could it be trusted? Did she even want to find out? Or would she end up back at square one, the way she already had when it came to Josh O'Hara?

Twice, in fact.

There had to be a limit on how many times you could go through that kind of emotional trauma and still survive.

The sensible thing to do would be to run. As fast and as far away as she possibly could.

* * *

Josh watched Megan making her way into the kitchen. The room instantly felt emptier without her which was ridiculous given the number of people milling about.

Not to mention a very large dog. Crash was being extraordinarily patient with all the small people who wanted to stroke his nose or try to climb onto his back but Luke was hovering nearby.

'Might be time we took off,' he said to Josh. 'I suspect all the Davenports are ready for a blast of fresh air on the beach. If we stay much longer, all these kids are going to start feeding treats to Crash and the consequences won't be pretty.'

Josh grinned. 'Fair enough. Thanks for bringing him.'

The noise level was rising steadily around them, with Shannon staging quite a spectacular tantrum, lying on her back and drumming her heels on the floor. Josh and Luke shared a grimace. 'No wonder you want to escape,' Josh muttered. 'It's enough to put you right off having kids, huh?'

But Luke just smiled. 'Bit late for that,' he murmured.

Josh opened his mouth but was too stunned for any word to emerge. And then it was too late. Small hands were tugging on his trouser leg.

'Daddy...*up*.'

Claire appeared in the doorway as Josh scooped Brenna into his arms.

'Who's hungry?' she called above the noise. 'And who needs some juice?'

Shannon stopped shrieking but the noise level didn't diminish as the tribe of excited, hungry children flowed past Josh towards the kitchen. Luke and Anna used the exodus as a means to slip away with Crash, and Josh watched them go, still somewhat dazed by their apparent news.

It seemed like whichever way he turned, things were changing around him on an almost daily basis. And they had been, ever since the disruption of his mother getting sick.

Ever since Megan's unexpected return?

That she was here in Penhally at all was surprising but the fact that she was still here at this party was startling enough to signify an even bigger change.

'Here…' Claire put a glass of sparkling wine in his hands as soon as he walked into the kitchen. 'Give that to Megan.'

'I'm not sure she'll want to stay long enough for a drink.'

His mother made a sound that Josh recognised from his childhood. He needed to do what he was told. With a wry smile he headed for Megan, fully expecting her to reject the offer. She hadn't wanted to come to this party at all and he couldn't blame her for that. Josh had expected her to drop in only long enough to be polite. To have a cup of tea and say happy birthday to the twins and then find an excuse to slip away from the chaos, like Luke and Anna had done.

But Megan looked more than happy to accept. Her smile was instant. Brief, but happy enough to light up her face.

'What a lovely idea. Thanks, Josh.'

'You're welcome.' The words were polite. They should have come accompanied by a smile to answer hers but Josh's lips felt oddly stiff. His fingers were tingling, too. Had Megan been as aware as he was of that tiny touch of skin to skin as the glass had been transferred?

There was certainly something very different about the way Megan was looking at him today.

About the way she was smiling at him.

Maybe the biggest change of all had happened a few days ago and was only now filtering through. He'd hardly seen her since that conversation they'd had in the cafeteria. Maybe because he didn't trust himself around her? If Brianna and her friends hadn't come in when they had, would he really have kissed Megan?

Did he still want to?

She was smiling again right now. At Claire this time, nodding as she raised her glass to her lips. His mother's expression was anxious. Did she like the wine? Was she enjoying herself? Megan's smile said that she did. And she was. The tip of her tongue appeared as if chasing an errant drop of wine from her bottom lip and Josh was aware of a sudden heat, deep down in his belly. He almost groaned aloud.

Yes. The answer was most definitely yes. For a long, long moment he couldn't take his eyes off Megan's mouth. God help him, but he'd never wanted to kiss anybody as much as he wanted to kiss Megan Phillips at this moment.

Megan's gaze suddenly shifted, jerking up to meet his as if she'd felt the force of that shaft of desire.

It was impossible to look away. To deny what he was feeling.

To one side of him, Brenna was climbing onto a chair, a mangled chicken nugget in her small fist.

'For you, Daddy,' she announced imperiously.

'Mmm…' But Josh couldn't move. Couldn't even look down. Not yet

Not when he could see that Megan knew exactly what he'd been thinking about. How he was feeling.

And she wasn't looking away...

A faint flush of colour had painted her cheeks again and her lips parted slightly. Never mind that the room was packed with people and there had to be at least a dozen conversations going on, adults helping little ones to eat or pouring juice or drinking their wine and chatting to each other.

Far too many people for such a small space and yet, for that instant, it felt like it had in the cafeteria days ago. As if nothing else mattered and he was alone in the world apart from Megan.

'*Dad*-dy...'

Josh lowered his head and obediently opened his mouth. The chicken nugget was posted home accompanied by a squeal of glee from his daughter and the moment was well and truly broken.

That flush of colour seemed to stay on Megan's cheeks after that. Was it the wine? Maybe it was due to the compliments that Claire kept heaping on Megan to anyone who was listening.

'She saved my life, you know. If she hadn't been there on the beach that day, I probably wouldn't be here, celebrating my grandchildren's birthday. She's my angel, so she is. Where's my camera? I need a photo.'

Rita was only too pleased to arm herself with the camera and take a picture of Claire and Megan side by side and smiling.

And then she wanted one of Megan with the twins.

'She was the doctor who saved them when they were born, you know.' Claire had to wipe a tear away. 'My angel, so she is...'

Josh stood back and watched as Claire engineered the picture she wanted. Brenna was happy enough to sit on Megan's knee but Max took a bit more persuasion. He was busy flattening chicken nuggets with his plastic Bob the Builder hammer. His grandmother bribed him by saying that he would be able to blow out the candles on his cake as soon as the picture was taken and in short order there was Megan with both his children on her lap.

Josh suddenly found it hard to take his next breath. Brenna was reaching up, unable to resist the urge to play with the tumble of Megan's hair. She seemed to change her mind at the last moment, however, and touched Megan's face instead. Unusually gentle for such a small child, Brenna traced the outline of Megan's smile.

Claire was dabbing her eyes with her handkerchief as Rita snapped some photos.

She was right, wasn't she? If it wasn't for Megan, this party might not be happening. She had been the person who had been there to hold them and care for them when they had taken their first breaths.

What a different picture that would have been from the happy, family chaos they were in the midst of here. Josh could paint that different picture in his mind all too easily. The bright lights and tense atmosphere. The hiss of oxygen and the beeping of monitors giving alarming readings.

How hard had that been on Megan?

Harder than it had been for him, banished to pace the end of the corridor and agonise over what might be happening?

Of course it must have been.

He'd begged her to save his babies, knowing that he couldn't face the agony of losing another child. But the child he *had* lost had also been Megan's and, although he'd done his absolute utmost to save the baby she'd named Stephen, he'd failed. And yet he'd expected Megan to do whatever she could to save the twins and he'd had absolute faith that she would. She'd made sure that he'd been left with the gift of life that he'd failed to give her all those years ago.

She must have been devastated at having to be a central player in such an ironic twist of fate. No wonder she hadn't hung around for Rebecca's funeral. She'd already done far more than it had been reasonable to expect and it was thanks to her that he had these precious children in his life.

And that he still had his mother.

His chest still felt tight and now Josh had a lump in his throat as well. How selfish had it been to harbour resentment at Megan for taking off the way she had? To have hung onto the anger that she hadn't believed him when he'd tried to explain the anomaly of sleeping with Rebecca that one last time? How arrogant had it been to assume she would trust him when he'd let her down so badly in the past? Turning his back on her after that first night together.

Failing to save *their* child.

And she had been afraid to tell him she'd moved on and become engaged to another man because she didn't want him to hate her?

As if the kind of love he had for Megan could ever, *ever* flip over to the dark side of that coin.

If anything, in this moment, seeing her here in his house, holding his children, he loved her more than ever. The power of that first night they'd had together was trickling back faster and faster.

Threatening to drown him.

A power that was becoming intense because this scene felt so *right*. Megan as the mother of his children. It felt as right as it had to create a new life together on the night they had been discovering each other for the first time.

But what could he do about it?

Too much damage had been done. Megan had finally taken definitive steps to move on from it all. What was it he'd overheard someone saying? Oh…yeah…she'd gone to the end of the earth in order to do that. And she'd found someone else there. This Charles that she was now engaged to.

Megan wasn't available so it didn't matter a damn how right any of this felt. He had no right to mess up whatever it was Megan had decided she wanted for the rest of her life. He had to let go.

Be happy for her?

But…what about the change he was so aware of today? The way Megan was looking at him?

Her smile…

The utter confusion Josh could feel seemed to be contagious. Max was suddenly overcome by the emotional overload of the exciting birthday party. He hit his sister with his plastic hammer and Brenna shrieked with outrage and then burst into heartbroken sobs.

Claire tried to rescue Megan but Brenna wasn't having any of it. She wound her arms around Megan's neck and howled more loudly. A kick from her small legs sent Max tumbling off Megan's lap and his face crumpled ominously. Josh moved in to collect his son. He picked Max up and held him tightly, making soothing noises to circumvent an additional meltdown. It would be time enough when things had calmed down to have a talk to him about what it was acceptable to use his new hammer on. It was certainly pointless right now.

'Maybe we'd better postpone the cakes,' Claire suggested, and there was a murmur of agreement from other adults. The twins weren't the only toddlers who were reaching the end of their tethers. The guests began to sort themselves out to go home.

Megan was on her feet. She had her arms wrapped around Brenna and she was rocking the small girl and making the same kind of soothing noises Josh had been making to Max. His son had now recovered his good humour.

'Juice?' he begged. 'Thirsty, Daddy.'

'I'll fix that,' Claire said. 'Can you give out the goody bags for everybody before they go?'

'Sure.' A glance over his shoulder before he moved to the front door to give out the farewell gifts showed him that Brenna was now almost asleep in Megan's arms. Her eyes were shut and a thumb was in her mouth. Her other arm was still wound around Megan's neck, though. There was even a small fistful of that tumble of brown curls, anchoring Megan's head in place.

When he got back to the kitchen, there were only a couple of guests remaining and Max was sitting at the table, eating pizza and staring hopefully at his cake.

'Later,' his grandmother was saying. 'It'll be our teatime treat.'

Megan was nowhere to be seen.

'She's gone upstairs to put Brenna to bed,' Claire told him. 'Maybe you could check on them?'

'Sure.' But Josh didn't return his mother's smile. Poor Megan. She'd not only attended a party she hadn't wanted to go to, she'd been firmly cast in the role of stand-in mother.

How on earth was she coping with that?

It had been a huge relief when Brenna's sobs had receded and the stiff little body she'd been holding had begun to relax. That boneless sensation of a child falling asleep in her arms had been so sweet Megan hadn't dared risk waking her by accepting Claire's offer to take her. Instead, she'd said she would put Brenna down for a nap herself.

To find Brenna's tiny fingers still clutching a handful of her hair when she eased her onto her small bed was enough to bring tears to Megan's eyes. She really hadn't wanted anyone else to comfort her, had she?

Kneeling beside the bed and leaning in close enough not to have her hair pulled painfully or disturb the toddler's slumber, she gently disentangled the connection, although she needn't have worried about waking Brenna who was deeply asleep now, her head sinking into her pillow. Dark eyelashes made fans above plump, flushed cheeks and a cupid's bow of her mouth made tiny movements as if sucking on something, even though the favoured thumb had been discarded.

For a long moment Megan stayed where she was, kneeling beside the bed. She smoothed some errant curls back from Brenna's face and then simply watched her sleep, marvelling at such perfect skin and the expression of such innocence that made sleeping children look like angels.

So precious.

So vulnerable.

The vice that squeezed her heart was all too easy to recognise and Megan had to close her eyes for a moment and try to take in a deep, steadying breath.

How had this happened?

How, in God's name, hadn't she seen it coming and put a better protective barrier in place?

It was too late now. She'd fallen in love with Brenna.

With Josh's daughter.

Megan heard the soft sound of movement behind her. Or maybe she sensed Josh easing himself silently into the room. Still on her knees,

Megan turned her head, knowing that her eyes were bright with tears. That her distress must be written all over her face. She loved a child who could never be hers. And now she was facing the man she loved and *he* could never be hers either.

She could see pain that mirrored her own on Josh's face. He murmured something that was inaudible but the tone was one of pure empathy. He held out his hand to help Megan to her feet and it felt only right that he didn't let it go. That he drew her into his arms and held her.

They were both suffering here. The swirl of their entire history, mixed with feelings that were too powerful to fight. And Megan didn't want to fight any more. She needed this moment. It felt right. As though there'd been something worthwhile in all the pain over so many years.

Because even a moment as perfect as this made it all worthwhile.

And then Megan moved from where her face was buried against Josh's shoulder. She turned her head and looked up to find Josh looking down at her. Neither of them could look away. There was something far too powerful for either of them to fight happening now.

Slowly…so slowly that she could have easily stopped it happening if she'd thought about it for even a nanosecond, Josh's head dipped and his lips came close enough to touch hers.

So softly. The love she could feel in that gentle touch was so pure that Megan knew she would remember it until she drew her last breath.

And then, faster than thought itself, the touch ignited and the flame of passion licked every cell of her body. Megan could feel her lips parting beneath Josh's, her body arching into his, a tiny cry of unbearable desire escaping her throat. A whimper of need that was so deep it felt like it was tearing her apart.

A tiny part of her brain remained in control, however. Or maybe it was Josh who was still aware that they were standing beside a bed that contained his sleeping child. It was impossible to unleash the passion but equally impossible to drag themselves away from each other. Every time they tried and the contact became light enough to break, they both pressed closer. Went a little deeper each time.

It was a familiar sound that broke the spiral.

Not the whimper of a child waking or the sound of someone coming up the stairs.

It was an electronic chirp. The sound of a text message arriving on the tiny mobile phone Megan had in the back pocket of her jeans.

A second chirp sounded as she and Josh finally stepped back from each other and the noise was just enough of a prompt to break the stunned immobility of the way they were staring at each other.

Megan read her message. She could feel the curiosity emanating from Josh. She couldn't meet his gaze.

A warning bell was sounding in the back of her head. Taking the shape of the thought she'd had what seemed like only minutes ago.

That things were changing and it was dangerous because she could get badly hurt all over again.

That the safe thing to do would be to run. As fast and as far away as she could.

'It's Charles,' she said, her voice totally without expression. 'He's waiting for me at the cottage.'

There was a moment's charged silence.

'You'd better go, then.' The words from Josh were as toneless as her own had been.

Megan still couldn't look at Josh. Nothing was being said and yet everything was being said.

'Mmm.' A strangled sound. 'I'd better.'

He wasn't watching her as she fled. Megan knew that without even turning back. He hadn't moved an inch. He was standing there, his head bowed, his gaze fixed on his daughter.

CHAPTER EIGHT

THAT KISS HAD changed everything.

Maybe that wasn't a good enough excuse for Josh to be where he was now, too late in the evening for it not to seem significant, standing in front of the door to Megan's cottage. But he'd been agonising over it ever since Megan had virtually run out of his house, according to Claire, stopping only long enough to snatch up her bag and jacket.

She'd left her cardigan behind, draped over one of the chairs that had been pushed to one side in the living room, and it had only been found when the children had finally been been put down for the night and Josh and his mother had been clearing away the remnants of the birthday party.

Returning an item of clothing wasn't much of an excuse, but Josh needed to meet this Charles.

To find out what his competition was like?

No. His motivation wasn't that juvenile.

Taking a deep breath, Josh raised his hand and lifted the brass door knocker. He rapped it briskly, three times.

He hadn't been able to think of anything other than Megan since that kiss. The kaleidoscope of memories, emotions and a determination to be honest with himself had swirled around and around in his head, sliding and colliding until *finally* they seemed to have fallen into place.

He had treated Megan abominably, he could freely admit that. He'd convinced himself he was being strong and doing the right thing but he'd been covering the fact that he was an emotional coward. And, yes, maybe he wasn't doing the *right* thing now but it was the honest thing to do.

He understood why Megan had left him when he'd been at the lowest point of his life, consumed by guilt at the death of a wife he'd never loved enough. Terrified by the prospect of being a solo father to two fragile, ultimately vulnerable, babies.

He had forgiven Megan for that. He had forgiven her for not believing him when he'd told her that his marriage was over. For thinking that he was sleeping with his wife at the same time he'd gone to Megan's bed.

His knock went unanswered. He could hear some classical music coming from inside the cottage but there was no sound of any voices. The thought that he might be disturbing something intimate prompted Josh to lick suddenly dry lips. To take another deep breath. He would try just once more. He rapped three times again, and then added another couple of raps, slightly louder.

The bottom line was that he could forgive Megan anything at all because…he loved her. It was as simple as that. And as complicated. He could even forgive her for marrying someone else and moving on with her life without him if he could believe that she would be happy doing that.

But Josh also understood why Megan had fled from his house earlier today, in the wake of that kiss.

It was still there.

Whatever they'd discovered on that first night together and rediscovered when they'd found themselves working together in St Piran's all those years later was still there.

Stronger than ever, maybe, because it had been denied and locked away.

Because of his stupid, misguided tunnel vision.

How had he ever convinced himself that he could only be the father he was determined to be for his children by denying love or commitment to anything other than them or his career?

He could never be the best father—the best anything, for that matter—without Megan in his life because he could never be the person he could be if he had her by his side.

He could never feel *whole* without her.

And, thanks to that kiss, Josh was convinced that it was the same for Megan, whether she was prepared to admit it or not.

So why the hell was she planning to marry someone else?

Just what did this Charles have that *he* didn't?

Maybe he was about to find out. The door was opening in front of him. Expecting it to be Megan, Josh felt his lips curling into a smile but the smile drained away when he found himself facing the man who had to be Charles. It was an effort not to let his face freeze into lines of… shock?

Whatever he'd expected Megan's fiancé to look like, it wasn't this. Charles was much, much older than he was. Pushing sixty? He had completely grey hair, wire-rimmed spectacles and… and he was wearing a *waistcoat*. He looked like he could be Megan's father. Or a favourite uncle. There was a kindliness about his face and his smile looked genuine but his eyes were sharp. This man missed nothing.

'You *must* be Josh,' he said into the awkward silence. 'Please, come in. Megan's having a bath but she'll be down in a minute, I expect.'

'I…ah…' This was so unexpected that Josh was completely thrown. Just what had he thought he would do when he got here anyway? 'I just came to return this,' he said, holding out the garment in his hand. 'Megan left it behind at the party. Perhaps you could give it to her?'

A hand was extended but not to accept the item of clothing. It was asking for a handshake.

'I'm Charles Cartwright,' the older man said.

'Megan's friend. Please do come in. I've heard so much about you, I'd like to meet you properly.'

Megan's *friend*?

He couldn't walk away now without appearing rude. Besides, Josh's level of confusion was rising. What kind of a fiancé described himself as a friend? Maybe Megan wasn't engaged at all and that was why she wasn't wearing a ring. Had she told everybody she was engaged to protect herself?

Perhaps all he needed to do was convince Megan that she didn't need that kind of protection. That he'd finally grown up and got over himself. That he could be everything that she needed him to be.

That it might not be as easy as it sounded became more apparent with every step Josh took into the cottage.

It was impossible not to remember the last time—the *only* time—he'd ever been here before. There was an air of redecoration chaos and a strong smell of paint that made it feel different now but nothing could erase those memories.

Steeling himself to do the hardest thing in his life.

Putting it off, just for another minute, resisting the urge to pull Megan into his arms from the moment she'd answered the door. Following her into the kitchen after accepting the offer of a drink.

And then he'd snapped when Megan had betrayed her nervousness by spilling the water when she'd tried to pour it. That kiss was seared into his memory just as deeply as today's now was but…they were so different.

The kiss in the kitchen that day, more than two years ago, had been one of desperation. A last kiss, before he had to tell her what he knew would kill the hope and love he could see in her eyes. When he had to say that he couldn't be in love with her any more.

And today's kiss? The only desperation there had been the need to get far closer than they could through a kiss. Far closer than their surroundings and circumstances would allow.

But they'd both wanted that, hadn't they?

The real difference was that today's kiss had been tinged with *hope*.

Or was he imagining that?

Josh's confused whirl of thoughts circled back and tried to start again. Why had he come here? What did he hope to achieve? The only thing Josh was certain about was that he was nervous. More nervous than the last time he'd entered this cottage because then he'd known what the outcome would be.

Now it felt like the rest of his life was hanging by a thread that was so tangled up he had no idea how to start unravelling it.

Charles was leading the way into the living area of Megan's cottage. It was cosy. The curtains had been drawn to shut out the rest of the world and the fire was a soft glow of embers waiting to be tickled back into life with some new fuel. A couple of wine glasses, one with a few mouthfuls of ruby liquid remaining, had been pushed to one side of the coffee table. The rest of the table was completely covered with photographs.

Josh had to step closer. To see what had been going on in this intimate atmosphere?

'Snapshots of Africa,' Charles said from behind him. 'Can I get you a glass of wine, Josh?'

'No... Thanks,' Josh added belatedly, knowing his refusal had sounded terse enough to be rude.

He couldn't look away from the photographs because Megan was in every one of them. Never alone, but often the only white face amongst a crowd of smiling colleagues. Or standing with family groups against the background of a tent city. Working in what looked like an overcrowded and pressured clinic setting. Mostly, with children. Treating them. Surrounded by them. Holding them.

'I brought copies of all the ones I thought Megan would like to have,' Charles said quietly. 'I'm a bit of an amateur photographer.'

'They're very good,' Josh heard himself saying politely.

But they were more than very good. The images were amazingly evocative. They captured the barren landscape, the poverty and suffering, the harsh climate so clearly Josh could feel himself stepping into that foreign world.

There was a profile shot of Megan, wearing her stethoscope, her head bent as she listened to the chest of a tiny child who lay in its mother's arms. One of those heartbreaking children who were all ribs and stick-like limbs and huge, huge eyes.

Megan's hair was piled up and clipped to the top of her head but some of that luxuriant tumble of curls had escaped, as it always did. The stray lock looked black—soaked with perspiration and glued to the damp skin of her neck and cheek. Josh could actually feel the urge to touch the photograph. To try and smooth that lock of hair back from Megan's face. To say something to ease the lines of distress he could see in her fierce concentration. In the lines of the way she was holding her mouth and the creases around her eyes.

He couldn't resist picking up another image. One that made him suck in his breath sharply the moment he saw it. He couldn't stop staring at it, even though he knew he was glimpsing something private. A picture Megan hadn't known was being taken because she was sound asleep, slumped in an old wicker chair, her head uncomfortably tilted so far to the side it was virtually resting on her shoulder, but still there was a hint of a smile curving her lips.

She wasn't alone, of course. Tucked under each

arm was a tiny baby, their faces so black against Megan's white coat and the blankets they were cocooned in. The babies were also deeply asleep and all three of them looked utterly at peace.

So *happy*.

'Lovely shot, isn't it?'

'Mmm.' Josh could barely produce an audible sound. He was seeing a part of Megan's life he could never share. A part of the woman he loved that was completely unknown.

'They're twins,' Charles told him. 'The girl is called Asha, which means Life. And the boy is Dumi—the Inspirer.'

'Special names,' Josh murmured.

'Megan chose them. She saved their lives when they were born and she fought for them every step of the way after that. Day and night for weeks, it was Megan who fed them and changed them and cuddled them when they cried.'

'What happened to their mother?'

'She came into the camp in the late stages of her pregnancy and it was too late to start any treatment for her advanced AIDS. She died within hours of giving birth.'

'And the babies?' Josh felt his heart sink like

a stone. 'Are they…? Did they…?' He couldn't bring himself to say the words. Megan would have been devastated if—

'They were lucky.' He could hear the smile in Charles's voice even though he didn't look up from the photo. 'We at least had the time to give the drugs that can help prevent transmission of the disease from mother to child. Neither of them were infected with HIV during the pregnancy and they were delivered via Caesarean and then bottle-fed, of course. They're both thriving.'

Thank goodness for that. Josh's relief was tinged with a sense of unreality, however. How weird was it knowing that Megan had been living a life that paralleled his own to such a degree? A lone parent figure for fragile twin babies.

'When was this picture taken?' he asked.

'Six months ago, when they were about eight weeks old, I think.' Charles sounded oddly hesitant. 'The twins were the main reason it was so hard to persuade Megan to come home and recover properly from the dengue fever. It would have been impossible if I hadn't suggested—' He

broke off suddenly, his head turning. 'Megan…
we have a visitor.'

'So I see. Hello, Josh. What are you doing here?'

Megan was dressed again after her bath, in
jeans and a warm pullover, but her feet were
bare and her hair hung down in damp tendrils
that she was still squeezing dry with a towel.

She looked…good grief…*frightened*?

Vulnerable, anyway. Heartbreakingly vulnerable. Because of him. Because he was here and
threatening to break…something.

Slowly, Josh put the photograph down. He held
out what he was still holding in his other hand.
The cherry-red cardigan.

'You left this behind at the party. I thought you
might need it.'

'Oh…' Megan came forward to claim the
article of clothing. 'Sorry…'

What for? The inconvenience of it needing
to be returned? Or for what had happened that
had made her flee his house in such a hurry that
she'd left it behind?

The moment was astonishingly awkward. It
was Charles who cleared his throat and tried to
break it.

'Megan's been telling me about all the fund-raising efforts going on for the clinic. It's a wonderful thing you're all doing.'

'It's Megan who can take the credit,' Josh said. He had to clear his own throat because his voice came out sounding oddly raw.

'She's also told me about the new paediatric wing for your emergency department. That's going to put St Piran's on the map in a big way. You've got a brilliant career ahead of you, Josh, by all accounts.'

Josh made a vaguely dismissive sound. Yes, he already had, and would no doubt continue to have, a brilliant career.

But it wasn't enough, was it?

Charles was clearly struggling to find a topic of conversation to break the loaded silences.

'And your twins turned two today? Megan tells me they're beautiful children.'

Josh managed to make another affirmative noise. Yes, his children were beautiful. They were everything to him and he would lay down his life in a heartbeat for them, if it was necessary.

But...right now...it still didn't feel *enough*.

He needed something more in his life.

He needed Megan.

At least part of what he was feeling had to be showing on his face. In his inability to even make polite conversation. No wonder Megan was starting to look embarrassed. Stricken, even?

'I'd better go.' Josh started moving but it felt like he was walking away too soon. That he hadn't touched on whatever it was he'd wanted to achieve by coming here.

'I forgot.' The words came out in a kind of a growl as he swung back to face Megan. 'We're doing a test run of the technology in Paediatric Resus tomorrow. X-ray and monitoring and so forth. You might want to be there to see how it comes together.' He tried, and failed, to smile. 'It doesn't matter, of course. If you're busy.'

The look that passed between Megan and Charles was palpably significant but Josh couldn't read the message. His gut was forming an unpleasantly rock-like mass inside him.

'I'll be there,' Megan said quietly. 'What time?'

'Three p.m. We're hoping that a Sunday afternoon might be a quieter spell. There are a lot of people who want to see if it's going to fly.' Josh forced himself to acknowledge Charles with a smile. 'You'd be most welcome to come too, Charles. You might want to see what Megan's been up to while she's been here.'

'Thank you, but I'm due back in London early tomorrow afternoon.' Charles was smiling back at him. 'And I've got a pretty good idea of what Megan's been up to. She knows I approve.'

Had there been some kind of hidden meaning there? Josh had arrived at Megan's cottage feeling agitated because he'd known something had changed. Or hadn't changed, more to the point, in the wake of that kiss. He was driving away feeling like he'd found more questions than answers.

There was a part of Megan he didn't know. The part that was bound up with Africa. That was *friends* with Charles Cartwright. A very important part. But he was missing something here, and he had no idea what it was.

Josh was still feeling agitated. And confused.

Totally at a loss as to what he could do about any of it, in fact.

* * *

The new paediatric wing of St Piran's emergency department was not quite finished but it was still crowded on this Sunday afternoon. The scenario being run of dealing with a child with multiple trauma after being knocked off his bicycle might be a pretence but to the medical staff involved this was no game.

From where she was standing in the second resuscitation area, Megan was close to the junior star of the show who was getting ready to play his part. Thirteen year old Jem, the son of Nick Tremayne, who was a Penhally Bay GP, had volunteered for the role.

'I'm going to be a doctor when I grow up,' he told Megan. 'Just like my dad. I'm already learning first aid. And I've done this for real, too, when I had my accident.'

'I remember.' Megan nodded. How could she forget? That had been when her path had crossed that of Josh's again so unexpectedly. A route that had only led, again, to an emotional disaster.

'I don't remember this bit of it, though,' Jem said sadly. 'I was unconscious.'

'That's what you have to pretend to be now.'

His father was helping one of the volunteer ambulance crew to fasten a collar around his neck. 'And no giggling. This is serious stuff.'

'OK.' Jem lay flat on the stretcher, closed his eyes and groaned. He tried it again, obviously hoping for a more dramatic effect.

Josh appeared though the doors leading to the main resus area. 'The paediatric trauma team have been summoned by pager,' he announced. 'On my count these doors will open and we'll take it from there in real time.'

He looked extremely tense, Megan thought. Not surprising, given that there were so many observers here. Word had spread fast. Albert White was here as CEO. There were quite a few of St Piran's consultant staff present, including Luke and Anna Davenport, and Nick had brought some of the other local GPs with him. There was also a reporter from a local newspaper accompanied by a photographer.

The tension was instantly contagious. Never mind any personal issues between them, if a major glitch showed up in this scenario, it could be due to a poor choice she had made about the design and predicted flow patterns.

It wasn't like Josh to be grim, though, even if he was stressed. He didn't smile at Megan when he spotted her. He practically scowled at her, for heaven's sake. So she'd arrived a little later than she'd intended. Did it matter that much? He was also looking less than amused by Jem's acting.

'Cut the sound effects, Jem,' he said briskly enough to sound like a reprimand. 'We can do without the groaning, OK?'

A minute or two later and they could hear Josh's count. 'Three, two, one…'

The doors swung open. Megan followed the stretcher that was supposedly arriving from the ambulance bay and pressed herself into a corner, out of the way. The paramedic who was helping started his handover, describing a serious incident in which a child had been struck by a car at speed.

'GCS on arrival was fifteen. Blood pressure was one-three-five on ninety. Resp rate thirty-six. Oxygen saturation ninety-nine per cent on air.'

As airway doctor, Ben Carter was leading the paediatric trauma team, consisting of other consultants, registrars, nurses and technicians. He requested another primary survey as soon as their patient was transferred to the bed.

The angle of the lights was checked, monitors switched on and trolleys moved closer. Megan could see the way Josh was following the movement of every person involved. He stood there, completely focused, looking tense enough to snap.

Findings were relayed via Josh, who was directing the scenario.

Strong peripheral pulses.

Pupils equal and reactive.

Tender abdomen.

Obvious midshaft, femoral fracture.

'IV line in and secured.' A registrar had taped a tube to Jem's arm. 'Hanging normal saline. Oh…where's the hook?'

An impatient sound came from Josh's direction as the minor missing detail was noted and fixed.

Ben was ordering blood tests and then X-rays. 'Neck, chest, abdomen and pelvis. We'll need CT on standby given the mechanism of injury.'

A nurse moved to test the phone lines. The X-ray technician manoeuvred overhead equipment. The staff were already wearing lead aprons, although no real X-rays were going to be taken. This was about testing the ceiling tracks and making sure that they could get the images that were needed quickly.

Josh stepped closer as soon as the process looked like it was not going to present any problems.

'The pelvic X-rays have shown fractures,' he announced. 'Your patient's now becoming restless and confused. He's vomited twice and his GCS has dropped below nine. Heart rate is rising and blood pressure is dropping.'

Ben nodded. 'We'll intubate prior to moving him to CT, then.'

Now they would all be able to see how well Megan's choice of positioning for equipment would work. The team had to pull in a ventilator and suction equipment, find ET tubes and laryngoscopes and draw up the drugs.

Megan didn't realise she was holding her breath until it became clear that everything was going like clockwork and then she released it in a long sigh. This was *great*.

The reporter thought so, too. He was scribbling madly on his notepad. The photographer was actually grinning as he took shot after shot.

Why wasn't Josh looking happier?

He almost seemed to be brushing off the congratulations that came in the wake of the successful test run.

'There's still a bit of fine tuning to be done,' Megan heard him tell someone. 'It has to be perfect before we officially open for business.'

'When's that going to be, Dr O'Hara?' The reporter pressed forward as people began to disperse.

'As soon as possible. You'll have to ask Dr Phillips. She's the one in charge of the project.'

The reporter nodded. 'And is it true that we've got a member of the Royal family coming to cut the ribbon? The Queen, even, or William and Kate?'

Josh managed a smile. 'You'll have to ask Dr White that one.'

But the reporter was distracted now. Behind Josh, Jem was sitting up on the bed, peeling off his neck brace.

'That was *so* cool!' he exclaimed. 'I could open

my eyes just a crack and see through my eye-lashes. I still looked unconscious, didn't I, Dad?'

'You sure did,' Nick told him. 'Good job. It wasn't scary, was it?'

'Nah.'

'What's your name, son?' The reporter asked. 'And how old are you? Can we get a photo?'

'Cool. I'll put this back on.' Jem lifted the neck brace.

'No, just hold it. Let's get your dad in the photo, too. You're Dr Tremayne, aren't you? What do *you* think of this new development at St Piran's?'

Megan decided to escape while she could. Why had Josh tried to deflect credit onto her? This whole project was his baby, everyone knew that. He'd been dreaming of it coming together for years now. Was he not happy with how things had gone today?

Where was he, anyway?

Ben Carter had gone back to his duties in the main department with most of the registrars and nurses who'd been involved in the practice run.

'Josh?' He shrugged in response to Megan's query. 'Hasn't come in here. He's probably lap-ping up a bit of the publicity. Hey…it went well, didn't it? Good job, Megan.'

She'd write a note, Megan decided, and leave it on Josh's desk. If he had a problem, he could come and talk to her about it.

The last thing she expected to find was Josh himself in his office.

No. Maybe the last thing was that fierce glare she was being subjected to.

'Sorry to disturb you.' She knew her tone was cool. 'I didn't think you'd be in here. I was going to leave you a note.'

'Why? Because you couldn't bring yourself to talk to me face to face?'

Megan gave her head a small, sharp shake. 'Don't be daft. I thought you'd be busy talking to that reporter or something.' The glare was getting on her nerves. She hadn't done anything wrong that she knew about. 'What's up with you today, Josh?'

'What's that supposed to mean?'

'You got out of bed on the wrong side or something. You're…angry about something.'

'Damned right I am.' Josh stalked across the

office and pushed the door shut behind Megan. He turned to face her.

'You can't do it.' The words burst out of him.

Megan already knew what the answer would be. Her mouth went dry but she had to ask anyway. 'Can't do what?'

'Marry Charles.'

She sucked in a breath. She'd known that herself last night, the moment she'd seen the two men standing side by side in her living room.

Her lover and her friend.

Her past and her future.

Safety…and danger.

Charles had known it all along, of course, bless him, but he'd been waiting for her to wake up.

Should she tell Josh why the engagement had been mooted in the first place? That it was no longer a realistic option?

No. Dammit. What right did Josh have to glare at her like this? To be telling her what she could or couldn't do?

So she didn't say anything. She just held Josh's angry glare. Her heart was thumping so hard it was probably visible. She couldn't move. Couldn't even breathe right now. The sheer *power* of this man over her was unbelievably stunning.

The moment stretched until it was unbearable. Josh snapped first.

'Why him?' Josh took in an audible gulp of air. He was rubbing the back of his neck with his hand—a sure sign that he was deeply agitated. The expression on his face was…desperate? He opened his mouth again.

'Why not *me*?'

CHAPTER NINE

MEGAN'S BREATH CAME out in an incredulous huff of sound.

'You're not available, Josh,' she shot back. 'And even if you were, you couldn't give me what Charles could.'

The words might be cruel but they were true. It was the reason her plans had gone in the direction they had.

Josh had flinched. 'Which is?'

'Security,' Megan said decisively. But then her voice wobbled and went quiet. 'Love…' she added.

Josh was gaping at her now. 'How can you *say* that? You know how much I love you. *I'm* not the one who's moved on.'

'I…haven't. I…'

But Josh didn't appear to be listening to her. He'd stepped closer. Megan bowed her head as he took hold of both her shoulders. She could feel the strength in that grip. The tension. And yet the touch was still gentle.

'Can you honestly say you don't still love me, Megan?'

She had to lift her chin. To meet a gaze so intense it burned.

No. Of course she couldn't say that.

She didn't need to say anything. Josh had always been able to read her like an open book. She couldn't look away. Neither could Josh. Not a word was spoken but it felt like a whole conversation was taking place. And the tension was leaving Josh's hands. His fingers moved, skimming her neck to touch and then cradle her face.

'Oh…Megan…' The words were a groan. Josh tipped his head until their foreheads were touching and they stood like that for a long, long moment. And then Josh pulled her into his arms. So close she could feel his heart thudding against her own. She could feel his lips moving against her ear.

'I *can* love you,' he whispered. 'If only you'll give me another chance. I've been blind. Stupid. I need you, darling. I want you. I…I love you. *So* much.'

Oh…*God*…

The words echoed in her own heart. They stirred up memories of similar words spoken in the past. And more… So much more. They stirred up memories of those intimate moments. The touch of those hands on parts of her body that had lain dormant ever since. The feel of his lips…and his tongue…on her mouth and her breasts and…*ohh*…the feel of him inside her. The absolute perfection of that connection that she'd never found—never *would* find—with anyone else.

How could she fight that, if there was even a small chance that, this time, they could make it work?

She couldn't. She couldn't fight. Couldn't protect herself any longer. She had to take this risk because if she didn't, she would always wonder if it *could* have worked. If cowardice had made her miss her chance of true love and as happy-ever-after as this life could offer anyone.

'I love you, too,' she heard herself whispering back to Josh. 'I always have. Always will.'

'Oh, thank God for that.'

They loosened their hold on each other just

enough to be able to see each other's faces. Josh still had a worried crease on his forehead.

'What about Charles? Your…engagement?'

'Charles has known all along how I feel about you, Josh. The engagement was only ever a…a means to an end, I guess. He's a friend, that's all. We weren't sleeping together.'

Megan's heart skipped a beat as the words left her mouth. She could see the effect of them on Josh. The knowledge that there was no barrier there any more. Josh wasn't married any longer. He was prepared to make a commitment. The children were being safely cared for by their grandmother.

He could take her hand and go home with her and they could go to bed together and make love. A fresh start.

The beginning of the rest of their lives?

'But… Oh, hell…' Josh groaned. 'Everybody around here thinks it was a real engagement. They'll blame me for breaking it up. There he goes again, they'll say, messing with people's lives.'

'It's got nothing to do with anybody else,'

Megan said. 'Except for the children, of course. And your mum. And Tasha.'

'They'll all be thrilled that I've finally come to my senses. They all adore you. Especially Max and Brenna.'

'And I love them, too, but…' It was all too easy to get carried away by the heat of passion, wasn't it? There *were* other people to consider here. 'Maybe we can wait until the dust settles,' Megan suggested slowly. 'We don't have to rush out and tell anyone.'

We need to be sure about this was the silent message she was trying to send. *So that nobody gets hurt.*

Especially her? There was no doubt that Josh was genuine in *wanting* to make this commitment but was he actually *capable* of it? Maybe there was no way to protect herself any longer but, by keeping it a secret, she could keep a shred of dignity if it went wrong. Again.

Yes…the fear was still there. Easily dismissed right now but would it ever go away completely?

I am sure came back in that intense gaze, but then Josh seemed to take a deep breath. Did he want some kind of insurance policy too? Did he have that same tiny flicker of fear? Whatever he was thinking, he was clearly happy to follow Megan's lead.

'Things *are* crazy right now. We've got the official opening of the paediatric ED wing coming up and there's still a lot to do.'

The fact that Josh was happy to agree to her suggestion made that fear flicker a little brighter but Megan doused it. She took a deep breath herself. 'And there are all the donations to pull together and get shipped off. I'm supposed to go and talk to Albert about that tomorrow. He's getting worried about storing all the stuff that's coming in from other hospitals.'

'And Mum's going to be tearing her hair out in the next few days if she keeps tripping over all the cartons piling up at our place.'

Yes. There was a lot to do for the next little while. It would be best for all concerned to postpone that fresh start to their lives. Maybe they both just needed a little time. To trust completely.

Josh was smiling down at Megan. '*We'll* know,' he murmured. 'And that's what matters, isn't it?'

'Mmm.' This *was* all they needed. A little

time. And then the fear would burn itself out and things would be perfect. Megan's breath came out in a sigh as Josh lowered his head to kiss her tenderly. 'I…I can't believe how happy I am right now.'

'Mmm.' Josh broke the contact of their lips for just a heartbeat. 'Me, too.'

He hadn't been exaggerating to say that life was crazy right now.

And it was all so damn exciting!

Josh's life as a single father and full-time clinician had always been quite hectic enough, especially at this time of year with Christmas approaching. This year Christmas was barely registering yet, despite the decorations beginning to go up around the hospital.

Everywhere he turned at the moment, people were telling him how brilliant he was and how proud they were to be associated with St Piran's. They also wanted more of him. His secretary was complaining that it was becoming a full-time job trying to schedule all the requests for interviews and television appearances that were being lined up to follow the official opening of their emergency department extension. Not only that, the media had got wind of the hospital's involvement in Megan's project for Africa and somehow he was getting way too much of the credit. He seemed to be becoming the face of St Piran's and people were liking what they saw.

Over the last couple of days Josh had been hounded by a television company that was trying to persuade him to agree to base a reality TV show around the new paediatric emergency unit.

'We'll do a re-enactment of the story leading up to the emergency,' the producer had enthused. 'We'll have all the drama of the medical crisis and then we'll follow up. Interviews with the family and the staff. Real emotional stories, Doc, and we won't shy away from the gritty stuff. We'd have no trouble selling this worldwide. You'd be a superstar.'

Heady stuff, but Josh wasn't interested. What he wanted was to have an emergency department that was renowned for its excellence. One that would be the first choice for any case that was within range of an ambulance or helicopter.

The local air rescue service was making noises about needing another chopper and more staff to cope with the expected increase in workload the hype over the new facilities was generating. He needed to slot in a response to their request for an urgent meeting.

On top of all that, there had been more than one fundraising event to try and attend. With space on a cargo plane already booked and the deadline rapidly approaching, it seemed like the whole of Penhally Bay and St Piran were at a fever pitch to get their projects completed and packed up.

Josh had a new anxiety as he drove home each day, that the stress of all these unusual activities would be too much for his mother so soon after her heart attack, but, if anything, she seemed to be thriving on it all.

'Dinner's going to be a bit late,' she apologised on this occasion. 'Rita's on her way over to help me with the last of the book bags. She was going to come after dinner but Colin's come down with the horrible cold the whole family's had and she's promised to help out tonight.'

'I can fix dinner, if that would help,' Josh offered. He could see that Rita wasn't going to be the only visitor to the house today. Megan came out of the kitchen in the wake of Brenna, who had heard her father come home and was rushing to greet him. Megan had a washcloth in her hands.

'Warning,' she called. 'Major stickiness coming.'

Josh couldn't have cared less about the sticky hands that were already in his hair as he picked Brenna up for a cuddle. Finding Megan in his house was becoming a regular event due to Claire's pleas for advice on co-ordinating all the community donations for the clinic. If his mother was aware of any change in his relationship with Megan, she certainly wasn't showing any sign of disapproval. Not only was Megan being invited into the house more often, she was being invited to step further into the lives of his children. Helping to feed them. Reading them stories. And more.

'Would you mind getting the children into their bath, love?' Claire asked Megan now. 'I'm getting worried that we won't get this last crate finished and the truck's coming tomorrow.'

Josh surveyed the train wreck of his living area. Max was sitting amongst a pile of beautifully decorated exercise books, trying to tear open a box of crayons.

'No, Max.' Claire rushed to rescue the crayons.

'Mine,' Max declared.

Josh saw Megan trying not to smile. She held out her hand. 'Hey, Max. How 'bout you come and show me your favourite toy for the bath? Is it a duck?'

'No.' Max scrambled upright. 'My *boat.*'

Josh looked at Brenna. 'Do you want Daddy to come and help with the bath too?'

'Yes. Daddy *and* Meggy,' Brenna shouted.

Max sneezed loudly and his grandmother sighed. 'I hope you're not getting Colin's cold,' she told him. 'Let me find you a tissue.'

The doorbell rang as she finished speaking and Claire flapped a hand in consternation, at a loss to know what to attend to first. Megan was really smiling now.

'Don't worry. I can sort the tissue.' She scooped Max into her arms before anyone could protest. Josh followed her up the stairs. He could hear his mother greeting her friend at the door, his daughter telling him something that made absolutely no sense, and even the strains of a

Christmas carol coming from the radio that was on in the kitchen.

It sounded like home. Family. And Megan was here in the midst of it all.

A taste of the future?

Megan looked up from turning on the taps as he entered the bathroom. She caught his gaze and her own face lit up.

She understood perfectly.

In no time at all the bath contained two very happy toddlers, who were splashing and crowing with delight as Megan soaped their plump little bodies and then tipped buckets of warm water over them to rinse off the suds. The splashing was getting vigorous enough to make the adults kneeling beside the tub distinctly damp. Stray curls of Megan's hair were sticking to her face and Josh could feel damp strands of his own hair flopping into his eyes. He pushed them back.

'I need a haircut,' he muttered. 'Goodness only knows how I'm going to fit in an appointment before the opening.' His fingers rubbed his jaw as he dropped his hand. 'And I'm going to have to find time to shave more often.'

'You look great.' Megan slanted him a look

that ignited a slow burn somewhere deep inside. 'When they see you on telly, women all over the country will be whimpering.'

Josh smiled back. 'Whimpering, huh?' He only had to tilt his body slightly for his shoulder to come into contact with Megan's body.

The eye contact had caught and was holding. Sending some very clear messages.

Oh…help… How long could they keep this up? This knowing that they had made a commitment to each other? That they wanted each other so much that it hurt? The anticipation that was building might be delicious but it was becoming unbearable.

It was just as well Max sneezed again at that point.

'Time to get you out, captain.' Josh caught the plastic tugboat in Max's hands just before it got smacked onto the water to create another satisfying splash. 'Small boys who are coming down with colds need to be tucked up in bed in their PJs.'

'Good thinking.' Megan had a towel ready to wrap around the slippery little body.

Brenna had her arms up, ready for her turn

to come out of the bath. Josh wrapped her in a towel and started to dry her.

'Did Mum tell you that Tasha rang?'

'No.' Megan's teeth caught her bottom lip. 'I've been so slack...I've barely been in touch with her since I got back here.'

'You'll get plenty of time to catch up. She's coming over for the opening.'

'Is she?' Megan was guiding Max's feet into the holes of his pyjama legs. 'That's fantastic news.'

'It is. Alessandro can't make it but he's put their private jet at her disposal. Nice for some, huh?' Josh grinned. 'She said she was really coming because she wants to see you. The opening is just a bonus.'

'That's not true. She's just teasing.'

'I know. But she was really thrilled to know that you're still here. And I think she might have guessed about...you know...'

'Did you say something?'

'Not exactly.' Josh focused on doing up the buttons on Brenna's pyjama jacket. 'But she thought I was sounding unusually happy and demanded to know why. I said that things were looking up—that the changes at work were pretty exciting and that Mum had a new lease on life what with the African project. I…um…apparently wasn't very convincing.'

Megan smiled. 'She'll know soon enough. Everybody will.'

'Can't be soon enough for me.'

They had both finished dressing the children in their nightclothes. It was time to move but the pause button seemed to have been pushed again as they shared a long, significant glance.

'I'll get them into bed if you want to head downstairs and see how Mum is getting on. Don't want her overdoing things.'

'She's loving it.' Megan raised an eyebrow. 'I'm starting to wonder where she's going to direct all her new-found energy once this project is finished.'

'Don't worry.' Josh shook his head. 'Wait till you see what Christmas is like around here. She'll have more than enough to keep her busy and happy.'

Brenna had been listening, wide-eyed, to her father. 'Kiss miss,' she said clearly.

Josh caught Megan's laughing gaze. 'Oh, yeah…' he murmured. 'I'm planning to, don't you worry.'

Two days later, the contributions from hospitals all over Cornwall and from the communities of Penhally Bay and St Piran were packed onto a cargo plane and started the long journey to Africa.

Megan watched the plane take off.

She was alone at the airport. Claire would have loved to have come but Max was really miserable with his cold and Tasha was arriving tomorrow and all sorts of preparations needed to be made. There had been no way Josh could take the time to come with her either. The opening ceremony for the emergency paediatric unit was only a few days away now.

That was OK. Megan knew how important Josh's career was to him and making this long drive simply to see a plane take off had been purely sentimental, really, but the project had been hugely significant to Megan.

Life-changing, in fact.

If Anna hadn't come up with the idea in the first place and Megan hadn't run with it, she probably wouldn't have stayed long enough to not only deal with the past but to move past it into a future that was bright enough to blind her.

Was that why she had tears in her eyes that she had to blink away more than once on the long drive home?

Maybe it was partly due to this being the culmination of such astonishing generosity by so many people. It had all been a bit overwhelming, in fact. Especially when she'd seen Albert White early that morning. The CEO had handed her a large white envelope.

'Open tickets,' he'd told her. 'I know the consignment will get held up in customs and so forth for a while, but we know how much you'd like to make sure it gets to its destination and the board of trustees wanted to show their appreciation for the work you've put in over the last few weeks. It's a return airfare,' he'd added, 'because we're hoping very much that you'll want to come back. There's a consultant position in Paediatrics that's still available, you know.'

The envelope was still in her handbag but Megan had no idea when, or even if, she'd be able to make the long trip back to Africa herself.

Did she even want to now?

And what about that job offer?

Did she want to work full time again? Or work at all when she could be a full-time mother to the twins?

That they were Rebecca's children had become insignificant now that she'd opened her heart to Max and Brenna. She already loved them as much as a birth mother could have. You didn't have to give birth to feel like a real mother. Asha and Dumi had taught Megan that.

Another set of twins. A whole world away.

Would she ever see them again?

Why was it that making a choice had to involve some kind of loss? To be with Josh for the rest of her life was more than she could have dreamed of for her future but the joy was tinged with sadness as well.

Life was a funny business.

That sense of loss and sadness was still with Megan when she finally arrived home to a dark, chilly cottage. She flicked on some lights, contemplated lighting the fire but went to her kitchen to make a hot drink first. She dropped her handbag onto the table, ignoring the way it fell open and tried to spill its contents, and busied herself filling the kettle and switching it on.

The knock at her door came just as the kettle came to the boil and Megan knew instantly who it would be.

Any regret over losses made by her choices evaporated under the glow of joy as she went to answer the door.

Josh was leaning against the doorframe, his grin lazy and utterly gorgeous.

'I missed you today,' he said softly. 'Thought I'd pop in and say hello.'

'Oh…that's nice.'

More than nice. Megan was being backed up against the wall of her hallway. Josh kicked the door shut behind him with his foot an instant before his lips covered hers. She reached up to touch his face but found her hands grasped and held on either side of her head, also against the wall.

She was glad of the support because there was no mistaking where this kiss was going and she was melting inside at the onslaught to her senses. No way could her legs have held her up without some assistance.

Josh finally raised his head. 'I couldn't wait any longer.' His voice was hoarse with need. 'I haven't even been home yet.'

'You're with me.' Megan smiled. 'You *are* home.'

She could see the effect of her words as Josh's eyes glazed from the force of his desire. His hands were busy, undoing the buttons of her shirt. A second later and they were sliding inside her bra to cup her breasts. The shaft of sensation as his thumbs brushed her nipples was exquisitely painful and Megan couldn't see straight any more either.

'Not here,' she managed to gasp. 'Upstairs. Bed.'

'Oh, yeah…' Josh groaned. *'Bed.'* He scooped Megan into his arms as easily as if she'd been one of the twins and headed for the stairs. He didn't put her down until he was standing beside her bed and he didn't put her down on her feet. He dropped her, flat on her back, onto the bed and leaned over her, loosening his tie.

'Oh, Megan. You've got no idea how hard it's been, waiting for this.'

'I think I do.' Megan watched Josh hauling off his clothes but she didn't touch her own. Josh could do that, too. When he unbuckled his belt and let his trousers drop to the floor, her breath caught and Megan had the passing impression that it might be possible to die from desire that was *this* strong but even if it was possible, she didn't give a damn.

As the trousers hit the polished boards of her bedroom floor they made a noise that rapidly became recognisable as the ringtone of Josh's phone.

He made a very impatient sound. 'I'll turn it off.'

Naked, except for his underwear, he shook the trousers to extract the phone from the pocket. He glanced at it.

Megan could swear she felt the world stop spinning right then.

'It's Mum,' Josh muttered. 'She wouldn't ring unless it was important.'

Megan tried, and failed, to ward off a chill of premonition. 'You'd better answer it.'

He did. Megan knew that it was something serious as soon as he began speaking because Josh's voice took on the crisp focus that she'd only ever heard in the emergency department. When something important needed sorting out. The questions he was asking only confirmed her fear.

'When did it happen?

'How long did it last?

'Where are you now?

'Take his clothes off. Sponge him down with some tepid water. I'm on my way.'

Ending the call, Josh didn't pause for a moment. He was doing up the button on his trousers before he even turned back to Megan.

'Max has had a febrile convulsion,' he told her. 'Mum's called the ambulance but she's scared stiff. I have to go.'

'Of course. Oh, poor Max…'

She should be able to see this from a clinician's point of view. To be involved and caring but not panic the way a parent would. But she couldn't. The fear that gripped Megan was that of a mother, desperately afraid for her precious child.

'I'll come too.' Megan pushed herself to a sitting position. She tried to start doing up her buttons but her hands were shaking too much.

And Josh was shaking his head as he pulled on his shirt. 'No need. It's probably nothing. He's had a cold. This is most likely just an ear infection or something.'

But it could be something much worse. Meningitis? Encephalitis?

'Where the hell is my other shoe?' Josh was swinging his head, searching.

'Over there,' Megan told him. 'By the window.'

How could Josh be sounding like this? Like a doctor instead of a parent? This was weird…

Unless he could sense how Megan was feeling? Was he trying to push her back? To remind her that Max wasn't really *her* child?

That Rebecca was—and always would be—the twins' mother?

She had intended to get off the bed and help Josh find what he needed but Megan couldn't move now. She was frozen with something like horror. And there was no need for her to move anyway. Josh was moving fast. Totally focused on what he needed to do.

What he'd needed when he'd arrived here was the last thing on either of their minds.

It'll be all right, Megan told herself. As long as he kisses me before he leaves.

But Josh didn't stop long enough to kiss her goodbye.

He didn't even *look* at her as he rushed out of the door.

He said something but Megan would never know what those words had been because she'd been sucked back in time. To when she'd seen him again, an alarming number of days after they'd spent that passionate first night together. When he'd blanked her, as though that night had never happened.

It felt exactly the same right now.

He'd been about to make love to her and then, in the blink of an eye, it had been as though it had never been about to happen.

As though she hadn't even existed any more. She didn't *matter*.

She couldn't stay here, on the bed, with her shirt still unbuttoned and her hair a tousled mess. Megan did up her shirt, forcing stiff fingers into action, but didn't bother touching her hair as she went downstairs.

It was ridiculous to feel like this.

Like what? *Betrayed*?

His child was sick. Maybe seriously sick. Of course Max had to be the priority.

But she was supposed to be sharing his life. Why had he shut her out? He hadn't even *looked* at her before he'd rushed off.

She couldn't do anything to prevent that old button being pushed. The one that fired the emotions she'd been devastated by so many years ago. She'd felt so…used that first time. Used and cheap and stupid. Incredibly naïve and so very, very hurt.

What had Josh told her that day he'd come to pass on the news that Rebecca was pregnant? That his children had to be the most important thing in his life. The only thing that really mattered.

Apart from his career, of course.

He'd been far too busy to come with her today. Far too focused on the upcoming public acknowledgement of his brilliant bloody career.

Something far too close to panic was clutching at Megan now as she paced back and forth across her kitchen floor, her arms wrapped tightly around her body. There was no comfort to be found in the hug or the movement, however. Megan shivered. Her home felt cold and empty with the absence of Josh.

So did her heart.

This was exactly what she'd been afraid of. That she would put herself back into this space. Every step she had taken had made her feel closer to Josh. More a part of his family. That the future was safe from the kind of emotional trauma she *knew*, all too well, that he was capable of causing, whether or not it was intentional.

The panic caught and held. Spiralled.

What the hell was she going to do?

With a sob Megan collapsed into a chair beside the table. Her arms flopping onto its surface. Coming into contact with her handbag. Half-blinded by tears, Megan started automatically shoving the spilled contents of the bag back into place.

The last item her fingers closed over was a large white envelope.

With tears still streaming down her face,

Megan stared at it blankly. And then she remembered what it contained.

Her fingers trembling, she opened the envelope.

CHAPTER TEN

'SHE'S GONE.'

Josh O'Hara scowled at his sister. 'What do you mean, she's *gone*?'

After a sleepless night, during which Max had been thoroughly checked and declared to be suffering from no more than an ear infection, Josh had taken the day off work so that he could collect his sister from the airport and look after the rest of his family.

Tasha had been desperately keen to see Megan so she'd taken Josh's car and gone to Megan's cottage as soon as she could without offending her family. She'd been gone a couple of hours and had now stormed back into the farmhouse, looking bewildered as she'd made her startling announcement.

Claire came down the stairs, having settled the twins for a nap. 'That paracetamol has worked a treat,' she said. 'Max doesn't even feel like he's running a temperature any more and he went out like a light. He's exhausted, poor lamb, after such a disrupted night. I'm feeling the same myself, so I am. I'm going to make a big pot of coffee.'

She stopped speaking and looked from her son to her daughter and back again.

'What on earth's the matter with you two?'

'Megan's gone,' Tasha said. 'The cottage is all locked up. I went to the most likely car rental agency and was told she handed in the vehicle and her keys very early this morning. She ordered a taxi. To take her to the airport.'

Déjà vu.

Josh could feel the blood draining from his brain, leaving a confused maelstrom of questions.

Why?

How could she do something like this?

Where had she gone?

What the hell has just happened here?

Snatches of answers were trying to compete.

You blanked her again, didn't you?

When you got the news about Max, she ceased

to matter, when only minutes before she'd been the only thing that mattered.

He'd shut her out. Hurt her unbearably and she'd reacted the way she always had. By running away.

Surely by now she felt she could trust him? Running away was… It was verging on cowardly, wasn't it?

The blood was returning now. Boiling back as something like fury began to nibble its way through all the other devastating emotions swirling around.

Both Claire and Tasha were staring at him.

'Kitchen,' Claire commanded. 'We all need some coffee.'

Moving in a vaguely zombie-like fashion, Josh did as he was told. He needed to sit down, that was for sure. To try and get his head around this. Half of him was furious. The other half was numb. Stunned by a blow he hadn't expected.

Didn't deserve?

Maybe he did. For his past stupidity if not for how badly he'd handled this latest crisis.

He barely heard the chatter going on between Claire and Tasha as they made coffee.

'I'll do it, Mum. You sit down. You look exhausted and you've had a heart attack recently, for heaven's sake.'

'I'm fine. Or I will be when I know what on earth is going on around here to make Josh look like the world has ended. Out of the way, Natasha. Or make yourself useful and find some mugs.'

A chuckle from Tasha. 'You certainly sound like your old self. I'm sorry I couldn't come over when you were in hospital. I was feeling a bit sick myself for a few days there and we didn't know what it was.'

'You didn't say.'

'I didn't want to worry you. And I'm fine now, except for first thing in the morning.'

'Oh…' Claire dropped the lid of the biscuit tin. 'Are you…?'

'Yes.' The joy in Tasha's voice made Josh turn his head and tune in properly. 'I'm pregnant. Three months along now.'

'Why didn't you tell us?'

Tasha sat down at the table and sighed. 'I felt bad, you know? About telling Megan. Knowing that she can never have her own babies. It wasn't something I could tell her in a phone call or a text and…and I thought I could tell her face-to-face. Today. She texted me this morning but now her phone's turned off.'

'What did she text you about?' Josh demanded.

'Max.' Tasha closed her eyes. 'She wanted to know if he was OK. I told her everything was fine and I'd see her soon.'

'And?'

'And nothing. That was it.' Tasha shook her head. 'I could have walked past her at the airport without even knowing. Why has she gone? I would have thought the opening of the emergency paediatric unit was just as important for her as it is to you.' She opened her eyes and glared at Josh. 'This has got something to do with you, hasn't it? I know how much Megan loves you. Did you give her a reason to think it was all on again and then do something to show her that nothing had changed?'

It was Josh's turn to close his eyes. 'Something like that, I suppose,' he muttered.

There was a long silence. The groan from Josh broke it. 'I knew it was like this,' he said. 'I was right to want nothing to do with love. It only wrecks your life. Someone always gets badly hurt.'

'Oh, *rot*,' Tasha said. 'Alessandro and I are as happy as any two people could be, thank you very much.'

Claire had totally forgotten about the coffee she was preparing. She sank into another chair at the table, her fingers at her neck, playing with her silver shamrock. She looked troubled.

'Do you love Megan, Josh?'

'Yes. Totally. As much as it's possible to love anyone.' He could feel his face settling into grim lines. 'But what's the point? She's gone. Again.'

'Wasn't she engaged? To that man from London?'

'Charles?' Tasha sounded astonished. 'No *way*…he was just a friend.'

'Not any more,' he told his mother.

Claire nodded. 'It was a second-best thing, then. Like you and Rebecca.'

'What's made her run away?' Tasha asked gently. 'Do you know?'

Josh didn't answer. If he did, he'd have to take the blame, wouldn't he? And he wasn't the only one at fault here. Megan had run away. Blanked him back in the most blatant way possible. He had every right to be furious with her, didn't he? Not that he expected his mother or sister to buy into that. He was outnumbered here, he could feel it.

'If you don't know, you need to find out,' Claire said. 'For a bright boy, Josh, you can be a bit simple sometimes.'

'I would have thought you'd understand better than anyone,' Josh told her.

'What?'

'You loved Dad, didn't you?'

'Yes, of course I did. I wouldn't have married him otherwise.'

'You loved him enough to take him back, time after time, after his affairs. You believed it could work and he just hurt you again and again. Hurt all of us.'

'Oh...' Claire looked devastated. 'You were just a child. I thought I was doing the right thing, trying to keep the family together.' She looked ready to cry. 'How could I not see the damage that was happening?'

'Hey...I turned out just fine,' Tasha put in.

'Joshie was the oldest,' Claire said sadly. 'I

leaned on him. I let him see more than he should have seen about how tough things were.' She reached out to touch her son's arm. 'But you can't compare my marriage to what you and Megan have. Have always had, from what I've heard.'

'Why not?' It didn't bother Josh that his mother knew far more than he'd realised. Nothing mattered right now except that he'd lost Megan.

Again. Maybe for good this time.

'The love in my marriage was one-sided,' Claire said sadly. 'Rory was fond of me, certainly, but he didn't *love* me. The balance was too wrong and *that* was why it never worked.'

Tasha was nodding. 'If you have real love on both sides, it's like a see-saw. Sure, it tips up and down a bit but you can always find the balance and when it's there, it's like a bridge into another world. Not a perfect world but...' Her smile was misty. 'It's as good as it gets.'

Josh knew that world. It was the space he could be in with Megan and no one else.

'You know how much you love your children,' Claire added. 'What that's like.'

Josh's smile felt rusty. 'It's the best feeling in the world.'

'Well, love between parents and children is pretty much a given,' Claire said sagely. 'When you get that kind of love between people who choose to be together, it's different but just as powerful.'

'Yes,' Tasha agreed. She had her hand on her belly. 'And when you combine all the different sorts of love in your life, that's when the real magic happens.'

'Like the sun that can shine through the worst of any weather,' Claire said softly.

'Or at least dry the puddles afterwards.' Tasha laughed. Then she sobered and patted Josh's hand. 'You and Megan have that. Put the past behind you once and for all and start again.'

The numbness was finally wearing off. The fury was still there but part of it was being directed internally now. Josh knew exactly what he needed to do. What he *had* to do. But was it too late?

'I have no idea where she's gone.'

'I think you do,' Tasha suggested.

'And if you don't, you can find out, for heaven's sake.' Claire sounded impatient. 'Ring that friend of hers that she isn't engaged to any more. Find out what plane she got on.' She clicked her tongue irritably. 'What on earth are you waiting for?'

Bleached, bone-thin cattle stirred the parched ground and made the dust swirl. Fortunately, there was no breeze to shift it any closer to where Megan was sitting beneath a skeleton tree that offered only a hint of shade.

Back at the camp for less than twenty-four hours, she was finding it a struggle to cope with the heat and the smell and how appallingly tired she was. The flight had been incredibly long. Plenty of time to catch her breath and reflect on her knee-jerk reaction of escaping Josh.

Why couldn't she get past the automatic response? Maybe it had been justified way back after their first night together because she'd had nothing to hang any kind of faith on. Now she *knew* how much Josh loved her.

But she'd known that last time, hadn't she? And then he'd come to her home and told her it was over—that they could never be together. Because the welfare of his children had to come first.

And it had been the welfare of those children that had sparked this reaction. Did she really think he would have come back from seeing Max at the hospital to tell her that he'd made a mistake and he couldn't include her in his life?

At that moment, yes… Her panic had been caused by the fear of exactly that happening and the only way Megan had thought she could protect herself had been to somehow make it *not* happen.

And now here she was, having ensured that the worst-case scenario was firmly in place. The way she had when she'd made the mistake of not believing Josh when he'd tried to explain about sleeping with Rebecca again?

He wasn't even going to attempt to explain himself this time, though, was he? Megan had turned her phone on first thing that morning only to find her battery was flat. It was charging again now but unless there were texts or calls she'd missed in her travels, she wouldn't be hearing anything today.

It was opening day. The pinnacle, so far, of

Josh's career. He'd already proved he could push her away for the sake of his children and Megan knew his career came a close second in his life priorities. It would be almost dawn in Cornwall right now. Was he awake already? Had he had a haircut? Would he shave for a second time, maybe, before heading off to face all the cameras and lights?

Megan shifted slightly, to ease the pins and needles in her arms.

'You're getting to be big lumps,' she told the two babies she held. She kissed one grizzled scalp and then the other, earning a toothless grin from Asha and a wave of two chubby fists from Dumi. 'Big, fat, healthy lumps. How good is that?'

One of the group of Somalian women Megan was surrounded by, Fatuma, was crouched beside her in the shade of the bare tree, holding a child of her own. She looked up and smiled. 'Fat.' She nodded. 'Is good.'

Megan kissed the babies again. 'It is,' she said softly. Speaking in Somalian, she continued, 'Thank you so much for helping to care for them, Fatuma.'

'It is my honour,' was the reply. 'You saved my baby. I help yours.'

Megan nodded gravely. The exchange of gifts was respected.

For a minute both women watched the older children playing in the bare field near the cattle. They all held long sticks and there was a stone that was being scooted across the ground by being hit. Shrieks of laughter could be heard and it was a sound that could, temporarily at least, reduce the grim reality of these surroundings.

Still, Megan sighed.

'I wish they *were* really mine,' she said.

'They are the babies of your heart. They *are* yours.'

Megan nodded again. It was true. She had missed them so much. If she wasn't able to adopt them as a single woman and take them home, she would stay here despite the risk of dengue fever.

'Lots of insect repellent, I think,' she murmured.

Fatuma looked puzzled but then shaded her eyes to look towards where the sun was glinting off the corrugated-iron roof of the clinic buildings.

'Truck coming,' she sighed. 'More and more people.'

Idly, Megan followed her gaze. The truck was one of those ancient ones with a big wooden crate on its flat deck. A crowd of people stood in the crate, filling the space to uncomfortable levels. Not an unusual sight. What was unusual was a face amongst them that simply didn't fit.

A white face.

The truck stopped near one of the camp registration tents and the people spilled out over the back.

The heat suddenly seemed unbearable to Megan. She could feel a trickle of sweat gluing the folds of her shawl to her back. Exhaustion and jet lag seemed to be combining to make her feel very odd. Unwell, even.

Or maybe it was just because missing Josh was so painful it was like having part of herself ripped away. The pain came in waves and this one was strong enough to have her hallucinating.

Imagining that the tall, lean figure leaping from the back of that truck was actually Josh. That he had come to the end of the earth to find her. That he was striding towards her, flanked by an entourage of curious children, through the shimmer of heat and clouds of dust like some kind of mirage.

Blinking didn't make things any clearer. Lack of oxygen wasn't helping but Megan couldn't take a new breath because…

Because it *was* Josh.

Unbelievably, Josh was here. In Africa. Clearly hellbent on finding her. And as he got even closer, she could see the grim lines on his face.

'Megan Phillips,' he growled as soon as he got within range of being heard. 'Don't you *ever* run out on me like that again.'

This was the part of Megan that Josh had never met before.

Having released the pent-up combination of anger at the way she'd run out on him, fear that he might have lost her completely and sheer exhaustion from the hideously long journey, Josh took a deep breath and soaked in the relief of seeing her again.

Crouched on the arid African dirt, with a shawl covering her head and wrapped around her body, Megan was clearly a welcome companion for the other women who were so well shrouded only their faces were visible. Expressionless faces that were regarding him with barely restrained hostility in the silence that had fallen after his heated reprimand by way of a greeting for Megan. Even the children playing nearby were standing still, as frozen as everybody else by this startling turn of events.

'Y-you…you *c-can't* be here,' Megan stammered.

'Why not?' Oh…*God*…she didn't want him to be here?

The woman closest to Megan touched her arm and said something in her own language. Megan answered in the same language. The words were incomprehensible but the tone was clearly reassuring. Her companion got to her feet with graceful ease and, by some unseen signal, all the others followed her lead. The children still clustered around Josh were shooed away. Someone offered to take the babies from Megan but she shook her head, smiling.

When the crowd had virtually melted away, Megan looked directly at him.

'Isn't it the opening today?' she asked quietly. 'The new wing of *your* department?'

Josh merely shrugged. 'Ben Carter's looking after that. He was happy to cope with all the publicity and I was more than happy to let him have the glory.'

'But...' Megan looked completely bewildered. 'It's been so important to you. You've dreamed about this happening for years.'

Josh stepped forward and crouched down in front of Megan. He wanted to take her in his arms but she still had her arms full of babies. And he still didn't know whether he was welcome here or not.

'It's not as important to me as you are,' he said slowly. 'I've dreamed of being with you a hell of lot longer than having a paediatric wing in my emergency department.'

A spark of what looked like hope flashed in the emerald-green depths of Megan's eyes but then they clouded again. She seemed to be having trouble processing his words.

'The children,' she whispered. 'Oh...*Max*.' She looked incredulous now. He'd left a sick child to come here?

'Max is fine.' Josh was unconsciously using the gentlest tone he had. The one that was so useful to soothe a frightened patient or its parent. 'He's on antibiotics for his ear infection and he'd bounced back, the way children so often do. Mum's looking after them. And Tasha's helping. Getting some quality "auntie" time. And some practice.'

The hint wasn't picked up. He could see Megan swallow hard.

'You're really here,' she murmured. 'You came all this way. For me?'

'For you,' Josh confirmed. 'I needed to apologise for the way I shut you out the other night. I just wasn't thinking and I'm so sorry I scared you.' His smile was crooked. Self-effacing. 'I know it's not much of an excuse but I am a man. I'm not good at multi-tasking.'

A snort of something like laughter escaped Megan. Unable to resist touching her, Josh reached towards her face, wanting to stroke her cheek. His hand became hijacked halfway there, however, caught by a tiny, dark hand. The grip was remarkably tight.

'Hello, there.' Josh smiled at the baby. 'Are you Asha?'

'No. That's Dumi.'

'May I?' Josh moved to pick up the baby. 'I know what it's like, juggling twins.'

Megan said nothing. She was watching Dumi, who gurgled with pleasure and held up both arms when he felt Josh's hands around his body. Josh gazed down at the small face and felt an odd tightness in his chest when Dumi's face suddenly split into a wide, toothless grin.

'He likes you.' Megan smiled for the first time since he'd arrived.

'He's gorgeous,' Josh said. 'They both are. Beautiful babies.'

'My babies,' Megan said softly. 'I'm going to adopt them. That's why I asked Charles to marry me in the first place because I thought the process would be a lot easier if there were two parents available, but…I could still do it, I think. I'm going to try, anyway.'

Josh nodded solemnly. She'd been a mother to these babies since the moment they'd entered the world. This was the unknown part of the woman he'd always loved and understanding this bond she had with these babies only made him love her even more.

'It would be good for them to have a father, though, wouldn't it?'

Megan's eyes were wide. Watching him intently.

'My babies would love to have a mother,' Josh continued. Oh…help…could he put what he wanted to say into the right words? 'You love Max and Brenna, don't you? Enough to be their mum?'

Did she love the twins she'd left behind in Cornwall?

Did it compare with the love she had for this man, who'd traversed the globe to find her? A love that was threatening to overwhelm her?

'Of course I do,' Megan whispered. 'They're part of you. How could I not love them?'

'Snap.' Josh smiled slowly. 'And I've just found the part of you that I knew was missing.' He took a deep breath. 'Come home with me, my love. Marry me. We'll both adopt Asha and Dumi and bring them up with a big brother and sister.'

'Oh…' The words painted a picture of a perfect future. One that Megan hadn't even dared to dream of when she'd put her trust in Josh's new commitment. She gave her head a tiny shake. 'Whatever would your mother say if she found herself a grandma to African babies?'

'She'd be thrilled to bits,' Josh said. 'You know what she said when she was driving me to the airport?'

'What?' Josh was leaning closer. So close the babies they were holding were able to reach out and grasp the hand of the other. They both gurgled happily.

'She said I would be a better father if I was a truly happy man, and a blind person could see that I was never going to be happy without you. That I needed you. That we all needed you. *Make sure you bring her back*, she said, *for all our sakes.*'

He leaned even closer and Megan felt herself sway towards him. Over the heads of the two babies their lips met in a gentle kiss.

'I love you,' Josh whispered. 'More than I'll ever be able to tell you.'

'Snap.' Megan's voice wobbled. Tears of joy were very, very close.

'Give me the chance to show you. Every day. For the rest of our lives. Could you do that?'

Megan could only nod. She could do more than that. She could use every day of the rest of their lives to show Josh that she loved him every bit as much. Starting right now. She closed the gap between them and kissed him again.

How tender could a kiss be? How much love could it convey? How sure a promise of the future could it seal?

A lot, apparently.

Much more than enough, anyway.

On both sides.

EPILOGUE

A BIRTHDAY PARTY for twelve-year-olds was bound to be a noisy affair.

Especially in the O'Hara household, with so many blessings in the way of family and friends.

Claire O'Hara's knees were a little stiff these days, so she moved from where she was standing on the edge of the veranda watching the game of football happening on the lawn to sink down into one of the comfortable wicker chairs.

'You all right, Claire?' Megan came bustling out of the house, a bunch of carrots dangling from her hand but paused, concern furrowing her brow. 'Is your knee bothering you again?'

'I'm just fine, lovie.' She eyed the carrots. 'Are you heading for the ponies?'

Megan grinned. 'We'll never get the girls back inside for food if I don't drag them out of the paddock. Want to come with me?'

'I went up before. You'd better take your camera. The ponies are looking very pretty with all their plaits and ribbons.'

'Good thinking.' But Megan didn't move to rush back into the house.

She wasn't looking at her mother-in-law any more, either. A tall figure had broken away from the game of football and was coming towards the house. Even from this distance Claire could see that her son only had eyes for one person right now. She could feel the connection between the two of them, getting steadily stronger with every step Josh took. The strength of that connection never failed to take her breath away.

Was it really ten years since Josh had come back from Africa and brought Megan back into their lives for good?

Such incredibly happy years.

Oh, there'd been the anxious wait about the adoption of Dumi and Asha and it had taken a while but what a honeymoon, to have gone back over there and brought the new babies home to complete their family! Claire had stayed in the farmhouse only long enough to realise what a superb twin-wrangler and mother Megan was and then, with one of those lovely twists that life could suddenly produce, she took over Megan's little cottage for her home and it was perfect. An easy walk to the lovely beach that made it so perfect for all her grandchildren to visit.

Josh had reached the veranda now and he and Megan were just standing there, smiling at each other—as though it had been only yesterday that they'd fallen in love.

'Need any help?' Josh queried.

'You're doing great,' Megan said softly. 'You and Alessandro really know how to keep a bunch of small boys happy.'

'We've had plenty of practice,' Josh laughed.

Yes. The O'Hara children's royal cousins were here for this celebration. Three little boys in the last decade and Marco, Alessio and Rocco were out there having a wonderful time kicking the football with Max and Dumi. Even better, Tasha was in the house behind them, feeding the brand new and much longed for princess, Alandra, named for her father.

'I'm going to round up the girls,' Megan said. 'Anna and the others have got the table all set. How's Luke going firing up the barbecue?'

'I'm just going to check.' Josh turned away but

not before he'd given Megan one of those lingering kisses that always made Claire's eyes go all misty. He turned back once more. 'You all right, Mum? You're not sitting out here all by yourself, are you?'

'No. I've got company.' Claire dropped her hand to where she knew it would encounter the roughened fur of an elderly companion. Crash was nearly thirteen now and getting stiffer in the joints than she was but he was a part of this family. So were Anna and Luke and their two children. Six year old Chloe loved to tag along in the wake of the older girls and nine year old Ben was a keen surfer and a best friend for Max and Dumi. As close as anyone could get given the bond between the brothers, that is.

Claire had to blink more mistiness away as Josh and Megan left to attend to party business. Who would have thought that two sets of such very different twins could blend to become such a perfect family? Eleven year old Dumi stood a head taller than twelve year old Max already but he had a gentle soul and the whitest, happiest smile that brightened the lives of anyone fortunate enough to be within range. The boys adored each other.

Brenna and Asha were completely different, too. Brenna was a total tomboy and Asha as feminine as they came but the two girls had also bonded as babies and now shared the passion of ponies. How Megan found the energy to ferry them to pony club and events was astounding given that she had been working part time at St Piran's ever since all the children had started school. Josh was just as amazing. His career still seemed to be on an upward trajectory, with his skills as a consultant in such demand and a new book due to be published on setting up and running an emergency department. He still loved to work on the front line, however and somehow he found the time to be involved with the boys' football practices and matches. Somehow, Josh and Megan had found a balance. Professional, personal and parental and they could work as a team and keep everybody happy.

The noise level increased. Claire stayed in her chair with Crash at her feet as the party attendees streamed past her on their way to the food. She smiled and Crash thumped his tail as children and adults greeted him and 'Nanny Claire' on their way past.

'Are you having a good birthday, Max?' she asked her grandson.

'The best,' he said, pushing his mop of black curls back and grinning at her. Heavens, but he was the spitting image of his dad at that age.

And so much happier…

'To be sure,' Dumi added with a cheeky grin and the Irish accent he'd perfected to make his grandmother laugh.

It never failed.

Claire was still smiling as the excited troop of girls began to appear from where they'd been dressing up the ponies.

Behind them, she could see Megan. And Josh. Walking hand-in-hand.

She lost sight of them for a moment, as the girls swept past but then she saw them again. All by themselves for a precious moment, in the garden of their home, with the beautiful backdrop of Penhally Bay sparkling blue in the sunshine.

They didn't see Claire watching them.

How could they, when they both so intent on kissing each other?

With an effort, accompanied by the happiest of sighs, Claire got out of her chair to make her way inside and join the happy gathering of her family and friends.

Life was good, so it was.

* * * * *

Mills & Boon® Large Print
Medical

October

November

December

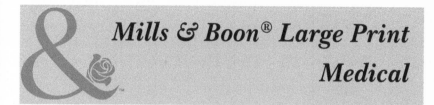